A gift for you. Enjoy!.

Neil Dolo[signature]

Blood
Oranges

GW00468057

Neil Doloughan

**Grosvenor House
Publishing Limited**

This book is published by
Grosvenor House Publishing Ltd
Link House
140 The Broadway, Tolworth, Surrey, Kt6 7Ht.
www.grosvenorhousepublishing.co.uk

A CIP record for this book
is available from the British Library

ISBN 978-1-78623-041-6

This book is dedicated to the outstanding work undertaken by the Emergency Services throughout the world: namely Police, Fire, Ambulance, Paramedic and A&E Services. They provide a dedicated service, often under extreme pressure and in dangerous environments. A lot of this work goes unseen and without the gratitude that is warranted. In Mallorca, this refers to the Guardia Civil, the Policia National, the Policia Local, the Bomberos de Mallorca, the Ambulancia de SVA, paramedicos and the staff of Urgencias.

Chapter 1

A Sense of Yearning

James sat astride his Vespa scooter and placed his retro-style helmet on his already slightly moist head and fastened the chin strap. He kicked back the side stand and pressed the automatic ignition button. His moped sprang to life and with a quick twist of the throttle, he was on his way. It had been a busy morning at the hotel, as it was most mornings, dealing with check-ins, check-outs and helping with serving guests their breakfast. Charlotte, his wife, was now at the helm and he had been granted the luxury of a few hours off to meet up with an old friend whom he had not seen for several years. He realised though, that in his eagerness to complete his duties before handing over to Charlotte, his rushing around had facilitated the formation of the numerous beads of sweat that had, without warning, appeared en masse on his brow and head.

As he left the village, heading in the direction of Sóller, the early summer wind was pleasantly warm and it aided the drying of his face, as he negotiated the various twisting bends. It was almost midday and he felt his scooter was the most appropriate mode of transport for getting around the valley. He made use of the family's car when necessary, for trips and school runs to Palma and for larger grocery shops, but James enjoyed riding his scooter when it was dry, which in Mallorca, meant almost all of the time. Riding any two-wheeled vehicles in the valley, whether motorised or not, was not without its risks. The roads and streets between Fornalutx and Sóller narrowed in places to one car width, and in a couple of places this was made all the more hazardous by being on a blind bend with only the placement of a convex mirror to assist road users. Some drivers either ignored these mirrors or were not aware of their existence, nor did they quite seem to understand the concept of directional priority road signs.

James, on numerous occasions, after being nearly wiped out by reckless car, lorry, bus and taxi drivers, had made good use of his limited Castellano and felt it necessary to vent his anger with outbursts of "¡gilipollas!" and "¡puta!" This was occasionally accompanied by an internationally recognised hand signal when the severity of the incident merited it. On a couple of occasions, drivers came so close to him that he could have seen the colour of their eyes if it wasn't for the fact they were completely oblivious to his existence and weren't looking at him. Their attention was being taken up with holding a mobile phone to their ear with one hand and attempting to control two tonnes of heavy metal at speed, with the other one.

He continued his journey, admiring the scenic beauty of the valley at every turn. He drove past the Cooperativa, over a little bridge at the edge of Biniaraix, into the back streets of Sóller and on past the Plaça d'Espanya, which was full of tourists and locals enjoying the delights of the small Mallorcan town. Sóller, now a mecca for tourists almost all year round, had a resident population of around 14,000 inhabitants, which swelled exponentially during the summer months. The town had previously had the honour of city status bestowed on it by order of King Alfons XIII back in 1905, a few years before the opening of the unique Sóller Railway. Visitors were able to enter the valley on an atmospheric, antique train from Palma, known as the Orange Express and were then able to take advantage of the valley's resplendent orange and wooden period trams, between Sóller and its port.

He followed the one-way system along the majestic, tree-lined and aptly named Gran Via and then out onto the main road, making the turn for Deià. As the road started to climb, James' route afforded him a spectacular view over the town and the whole Sóller Valley. His journey took him along a stunning road, which skirted the dramatic coastline of this part of western Mallorca. He made his way at a leisurely pace, allowing himself the pleasure of glimpsing the azure sea below with the occasional sight of a white sail or wake from various pleasure craft, as they made their way to Cala Deià or Sa Foradada, and he marvelled at various palatial fincas en route with their clifftop vantage points. He passed the iconic little hamlet of Llucalcari, with its cluster of grand old houses and majestic palm trees and then on into Deià itself. Traffic had come to a bit of a standstill as two coaches, heading in different directions, had met in the main street but whose journey had been somewhat curtailed by a rental car, having been abandoned on the street with its hazard lights flashing. James' prior experience of this type of abandonment made him sceptical that the car had actually broken down but rather he felt the odds were firmly more in favour of a lazy driver having nipped in for a non-essential item at the local shop. Sure enough, after several minutes of shouting, hand gesturing, pontificating and having to endure a symphony of car and coach horns, a rather blasé man appeared from the nearby grocery store. He sauntered nonchalantly towards the car causing the blockage, got in and drove off, without so much as a 'by your leave', to the bewilderment of all the previously irate drivers, who appeared to have been stunned into silence by the sheer audacity of the man. Normality was soon restored and vehicles passed freely on their way. James' journey continued through Deià and then beyond, as he headed in the direction of Valldemossa but turned off for its port. He had tackled the drive down to the Port of Valldemossa many times before; a drive from several hundred feet above sea level of about six kilometres, down a series of narrow hairpin bends leading to a small collection of former fisherman's cottages, with a pebble beach and a little harbour. He had done it with his family and in a car but on the scooter it was much more exhilarating and the tight turns were more easily approached.

He arrived and rode past the two small waterfront cafés and saw his friend already seated at a table, who waved at him on recognising his distinctive retro moped. James parked his scooter in the 'motos bay' a few metres away, took off his helmet and walked the short distance to where his friend was now standing to greet him.

"Well look at you! This life is certainly suiting you. You have lost a little weight, no? You are, what is the correct way of saying this; buff?" asked Ramon, with a broad grin backed up with a handshake, which morphed into a full hug. Both men instinctively realised that a handshake was too formal a greeting for old friends who, although had sporadically kept in touch by phone messages or social media, had not seen each other for about three years.

"Ramon! How the hell are you?" retorted James, on being released from his firm hug.

"Bien, bien, super bien. ¿Y tu?" he replied.

"¡Estoy muy bien amigo, pero mi Españyol todavia no es muy bueno!" said James, admitting that his Spanish language skills still left a lot to be desired.

"Don't worry, my friend, it will come in good time. What will you have to drink?" asked Ramon, beckoning the waiter over.

"Una caña para mí," said James to the waiter, sitting down.

"Y otro mas," said Ramon, handing the waiter his empty beer glass.

"Well, first and foremost, congratulations on your promotion...again," said James.

"Oh, thank you, thank you," replied Ramon, shaking his head and waving his hand, as if to say it was no big deal.

"So how was Barcelona?" asked an intrigued James.

"Barcelona is Barcelona. It is a unique, fantastic city. It is where I grew up but it is like any big city all over the world, as far as crime is concerned. You know what I am talking about amigo. You have worked in London and in Belfast. Sometimes, when you know too much of what goes on in a place, it can distort your view of that place. It will always have a special place in my heart but I am not sad to leave it. My wife and boys are also glad to be back here in Mallorca, and if we left it any later, it would have been unsettling for the boys. They have gone back to their old school and have picked up the friendships that they had from three years ago, so all is good. Ah here we go," said Ramon, as the waiter placed the two beers on the table.

"A toast to my good friend, James Gordon, to his resilient and understanding family, and to our friendship. ¡Salud!"

"¡Salud!" said James, before taking several gulps of his chilled, refreshing beer.

"How are Charlotte and the boys?" enquired Ramon.

"They are all good. Charlotte is busy with me in the hotel and Adam is doing okay at Belver. Reuben has settled in well and is now pretty much tri-lingual. In fact, he makes fun of how poor my Spanish is, and as for my Catalan, well that's another story. I have started an online Spanish course at long last and I'm enjoying it, so give me a year and you should see a big improvement.

"But listen, well done on your second promotion in three years. What rank are you now?" asked James.

"I am now officially Comisario of a specialist unit – The UDYCO or Unidad de Droga y Crimen Organizado. Basically our unit investigates drugs and organised crime here in Mallorca. I officially start next week, although I went in briefly last week to meet my team but for now I am on leave just enjoying this beautiful island. We have rented a nice apartment just behind Paseo Marítimo in Palma, which is close to my work, but we thought we would come and spend a few days here in Port de Valldemossa as a friend of Marta's owns a little house just round the corner with great sea views. The boys have been coming back from school and we have been swimming, exploring and eating good food. Did you know my wife is a great cook? You and Charlotte have to come and see us in Palma and bring the boys too. She does the best 'frito mallorquín' and her 'arròs brut' is magnífico. You know these dishes?" asked Ramon.

"Yes, yes I like them both. That would be great," said James.

The two men chatted over several more small beers and arranged a dinner date for both families in Palma, towards the end of the month, before James bid his friend farewell and headed back to Fornalutx. It had been a very pleasant afternoon for him and he was glad that Ramon was back working and living in Mallorca.

His first meeting with Ramon had been almost four years previously, after James had discovered the murdered body of an expat criminal who had been hiding out in a house in Fornalutx. James had agreed to help the local police with their enquiries and it was at Sóller Police Station that he first met the initially brusque Inspector Ramon Martinez. James and his family went through a great deal over the subsequent weeks, including his son Adam being kidnapped by Danny Kusemi, a notorious criminal from Bermondsey, South London, after James had inadvertently discovered a large stash of Kusemi's stolen proceeds of crime.

Kusemi had attempted to kill James in his own home but James had managed to overpower him and Kusemi was subsequently arrested and charged with murder, attempted murder and various other offences and was due to serve a life sentence in a Spanish prison only to be killed by the Russian mafia, to whom he owed the money. James had narrowly avoided being shot by one of their hitmen, as he had become embroiled in a criminal vendetta through the actions of his friend Matt. Throughout this whole process, Ramon had been at hand to provide support and police protection and James had repaid Ramon by helping him solve two major crimes within the Sóller Valley. James' actions had been recognised by being awarded the Medalla al Mérito de la Protección Civil after being put forward for this prestigious award by Ramon and his boss. As an ex-police officer, James had something in common with Ramon, but as a man he had shared some major traumas with him and he now had a special bond with him.

Life in The Sóller Valley had been quiet, as far as crime was concerned, over the subsequent three years since Ramon had left Mallorca on promotion to a new posting to Barcelona. James had been busy with running Hotel Artesa in Fornalutx and *Soul*, his houseboat in Palma Marina: a rest and recuperation getaway for serving police officers suffering from physical or stress-related injuries. Although James was glad to no longer be a serving police detective, he was keen to find out about whatever cases Ramon was prepared to disclose to him. This was something that had been missing from his life since Ramon's departure and which he had not realised, until meeting his friend again, just how much he had actually missed it.

Chapter 2

Aces High

A few days later, after catching up with Ramon, James' alarm unceremoniously announced that it was time to get up. Charlotte was already up and would be preparing breakfast for their guests next door at their small hotel. He jumped out of bed with extra vigour as he remembered today was hopefully not going to be a usual kind of day. It was 7.30am and Reuben, James' younger son, was already washed and dressed and sitting at the breakfast table, as was the norm. Reuben was very grown up and responsible for a nine year old when it came to any matters concerning school. He did not like to be late for school and so, was regimented in his morning routine in getting up in good time by himself and getting his own breakfast. His older brother was a different kettle of fish, so James knocked on Adam's bedroom door and he heard him stir. After a quick shower, he dressed and joined Reuben at the breakfast table.

"Only two more days to go, Reuben. Will you be doing much for the next couple of days at school?" he asked.

"Not really. Cata said we could bring in some games tomorrow. By the way Dad, we are going on a trip today to s'Albufera Nature Reserve, so I need to take a packed lunch. Remember, Dad?" asked Reuben.

"Oh that's right. I forgot about that, I mean I nearly forgot about that. Right, I will make you something now for lunch and you will need something for your 'berenar' as well," said James.

"Dad!" said Reuben, shaking his head.

James started to prepare Reuben's packed lunch, feeling a little put out after being admonished by a nine year old, when Adam appeared in the kitchen and pulled out a chair at the table.

"Morning," he said with a yawn, sitting down.

"Morning. Right, Adam you sort yourself out please and we need to leave in fifteen minutes. The traffic has been bad the last couple of days and I don't want to always have to rush," said James.

"Fine. Okay," he responded.

"I need to be back from Palma in good time today because I'm going to meet a celebrity," said James, emphasising the word 'celebrity' and waiting for a response.

He didn't have long to wait as both boys looked round simultaneously with interest at the word 'celebrity' and Adam, nearly choking on his cereal asked,

"Really? Which celebrity? Come on Dad, are you joking?"

"No, I'm not joking. It is someone you both will have seen on TV before but I'm not going to tell you until later, in case it doesn't happen."

"Aw come on Dad, why can't you tell us now?" pleaded Reuben.

"Probably because he's making it up," said Adam forcefully, spitting pieces of cereal out in an effort to make his point.

"Adam!" said James sternly. "Don't speak with your mouth full, and secondly, why would I make it up? I don't want to tell you until after I've met the guy. He is extremely busy and I'm only going because Glen asked me to go with him. It's really him who's meeting this person as a special birthday present for his fiftieth that Linda, his wife, organised. So there's no guarantee I will meet him, so just wait until later and I'll tell you all about it, so, ¡venga! ¡Va vamos!" said James, clapping his hands together to gee up the two boys.

"At least we know it's a man," said Adam, throwing his schoolbag over his shoulder.

"I think I know who it is," said Reuben smiling.

"Tell me! Tell me!" shouted Adam.

"I'm not sure," said Reuben coyly. "No, I actually don't have any idea who it is."

Reuben put his rucksack on his back and started to make his way out the door to the bus stop a short distance away that would take him and several other children from Fornalutx to their school Es Puig, in neighbouring Sóller, before James shouted,

"Wait Reuben! Your packed lunch."

James placed it, along with his son's drinks bottle, in Reuben's rucksack before giving him a kiss and saying,

"Have a good day and I promise to tell you later. Bye."

"Right Adam, give your hair a bit of a brush before we go anywhere. Did you have a shower this morning?" said James in an exasperated tone.

"It's alright, Dad," replied Adam, wiping a hand over his hair in an attempt to placate his father, before seeing James' expression of 'really?' made him retort with a 'Grrr!' sound, followed up with,

"Alright then!" as he wandered into the shower room and gave his hair literally two strokes with a hairbrush as James looked on, before edging past his father and making his way towards the front door saying,

"It's fine. I thought you didn't want to be late," with a degree of sarcasm only a teenager could muster.

After dropping his son off at Belver International School in Marivent, Palma, James drove straight back to Fornalutx and parked the car. He walked up to the central village plaça, where he had arranged to meet his friend Glen for a coffee, before heading off to meet the celebrity. Glen was already sipping a coffee at a table outside Ca'n Benet, a local café bar.

"Are you not getting changed? Here, what do you want? I'll get these," he said.

"Un café con leche," James shouted inside, towards Toni, the owner.

"Vale," came the reply.

"I'll get ready after this. I didn't want to give the game away to the boys because I haven't told them who we're seeing. We've got time haven't we? What time do we need to be there for?" asked James.

"Well, Linda said we need to be there for about eleven-thirty but I'm not exactly sure where I'm going, so I want to leave in about half an hour if that's okay," answered Glen.

"Of course. It's your present. I'm just pleased you asked me to accompany you, so I'll neck my coffee when it comes and go and get changed and then we'll go," said James.

Glen was a friend of James', who was also from Northern Ireland but whom he had only met since coming to Fornalutx. Glen and his wife Linda had owned a house in the village for about ten years and although they still lived in Northern Ireland they made frequent visits to their property in the village and were contemplating a permanent move there in the near future. Glen was one of James' tennis partners and his wife, an interior designer, had recently finished the interior of the renowned golfer Rory McIlroy's Holywood apartment, just outside of Belfast, and she had got to know him quite well. Realising that her husband's fiftieth birthday was coming up, and knowing that Rory was friendly with Mallorca's very own tennis legend, Rafa Nadal, Linda called in a huge favour for her tennis-loving husband, and as a result both Glen and James – subject to the time constraints of Rafa – were due to have a knock about with him at his newly opened, state-of-the-art Rafa Nadal Tennis Academy at his home town of Manacor, in the centre of the island.

James' coffee arrived and he took a generous sip. He watched as Glen was engrossed with his expensive-looking Olympus camera.

"Expecting some action shots of your winners against Rafa are we?" he said with a rueful grin.

"Yeah, as if. I will be happy just to be able to make a few returns but it would be nice to have a few action shots of us playing as well as a few of me just hanging around with my 'besie mate' Rafa. Also, if you wouldn't mind maybe taking a video of us playing on my mobile phone?" asked Glen.

"I'm sure I could manage that," replied James.

"I just think it is really nice of the guy to take time out of his extremely busy schedule to meet me, a guy he has never met before, whether it's for a significant birthday or not, just because his friend Rory has asked him as a big favour. I thought about getting him a special present as a thank you, but what do you give a multi-millionaire sporting legend who has pretty much everything he could ever want?" asked Glen.

"A year's supply of potato bread and Tayto cheese and onion crisps?" said James, raising his eyebrows.

"Oh yeah, I'm sure he would definitely think he was playing with a real McCooey then!" laughed Glen. "No, in all seriousness, I'm going to send him something special afterwards as a thank you; I just don't know what yet," said Glen grinning.

"Anyhoo! I'm ready when you are. I'm just going to nip up and change and I'll see you here in five minutes. Think I'll put on my special budgie smuggler Lycra shorts and my Gold's Gym stringer vest for the occasion," said James with a wry smile. "Oh, and I will definitely be asking him did he really shout 'New balls please' when he hit Andy Murray in the groin during practice last year at the Australian Open."

Glen laughed nervously whilst playing with his camera.

A short time later both men, resplendent in their best tennis gear, set off for Manacor and their meeting with their sporting hero.

Several hours later, Charlotte was at the reception desk, as the door of Hotel Artesa opened as James entered, walked up to her and kissed her on the cheek.

"You stink of beer! And fags!" she said assertively, as she recoiled slightly before adding, "Well go on then, how was it? Did you get to play with him? Did Glen enjoy it?"

James, with a smug look and slightly swaying from his post-tennis liquid lunch, after stopping off again in the plaça in Fornalutx with Glen to celebrate their meeting with Rafa, said,

"Yeah, it was alright," in a matter-of-fact tone, before quickly adding,

"I'm kidding. It was brilliant! You know I am not the sort of guy who normally gets star-struck but he is such a nice guy and he even played *me* three games of tennis! It's a fantastic set-up he has there. The tennis academy is brand spanking new. We were both really nervous about meeting him but he was so casual. He knows Josep from Fornalutx and he's a friend of Juan, the tennis coach from Sóller Tennis Club. Anyway, he played a set with Glen, who played really well by the way but Rafa beat him 6-2. Rafa was taking it fairly easily but they are both competitive guys, so when Glen won the first game, I could see Rafa step it up a gear. I had a knock up with him and then played my three games, which I have to say he won 3-0 but I took him to deuce in one of them, but guess what?" said an expectant and smiling James.

"What?" asked Charlotte, deliberately delaying before she spoke.

"I served two consecutive aces against Rafael Nadal! Fourteen-time Grand Slam winner beaten by two aces from James Gordon – about fourteen-times player from Fornalutx. Back of the net! Or over the net or something about the net! To be fair, I followed it up with two double faults at the thought of winning a game and choked," laughed James.

"How many beers have you had?" tutted Charlotte, although she was secretively enamoured to see that James had obviously enjoyed the experience.

"We only had three or four. I'm absolutely fine. I'm just on a high after my match. Oh, Glen videoed my games on his mobile and he will send it to me later, so you can see how it went for yourself and I can show the boys. But what a really lovely bloke to do that for Glen as a favour to Rory McIlroy and to then play me, so I felt part of it too. Glen's still down at the square trying to work out what to send him as a thank you and not getting very far, but that's me, I'm done. I'm off home to tell the boys. Bye!"

Charlotte shook her head, realising from previous experience that she may not get as much sleep as she would like later that night, as James had a tendency to snore loudly after consuming alcohol.

She returned home an hour later from the hotel next door, to find James still recounting his experience to both their boys around the supper table and she noticed that James was now sporting a new tennis shirt and cap with 'Rafa Nadal Academy' emblazoned on both. After dinner, James headed upstairs to take a shower but after he hadn't returned after an hour Charlotte decided to go upstairs to check on him, only to find him asleep in bed and snoring, as she had predicted. It had been a good day.

Chapter 3

When Two Worlds Collide

The summer season was well under way and the Valley of the Oranges had received its usual plethora of visitors with open arms. Hotel Artesa had full occupancy, with most guests being easy to please, and for the most part it was a rewarding experience for James. He was eager to share his local knowledge of all that the area had to offer and to provide tips about places to see, or give his clientele restaurant recommendations, in an effort to allow them to enjoy their holiday to the fullest extent. However, several days previously, an American couple in their sixties had checked into the hotel for a week and from the outset James got the feeling that these people would be challenging. Harvey and Ruth were from New York State, which they were evidently very proud of as they kept telling this to the other guests. Initially James found their loud voices and strong accents quite endearing, especially when they asked for a 'cup a cawfee'. He felt as if he was on the set of *Cagney & Lacey*. However, as the days went by, their initial quirkiness and loud demands started to wear thin. Harvey, who never seemed to pause for breath, had a wardrobe that could only be described as Liberace meets The Beach Boys.

Their first complaint was that the cleaners had obviously turned off their air conditioning when turning down their beds each evening. They stipulated that the room temperature was twenty-three degrees when they turned in for the night and that they had to have the room temperature at twenty-two degrees for Ruth at all times. James tried to play the environmental card but this had no effect so the cleaners were instructed to leave the air conditioning on at all times.

They had arrived by taxi and had not hired a car for the duration of their holiday as "Harv finds it difficult to get around on anything other than freeways", so they were dependent on the local Fornalutx taxi drivers to get out of the village. The protocol in Mallorca regarding taxis was that you must use a local taxi from where you are departing, so at busy times, there was likely to be a delay and one thing Harvey and Ruth didn't like to do, was wait. After a couple of episodes, James suggested that they book a Fornalutx taxi in advance. It wasn't a problem getting back from other places, as there were sufficient taxis operational. Although the bus service from Fornalutx was more frequent in the summer, none of the times seemed to suit the pair and their inability to 'hail a cab' was becoming their main topic of conversation with fellow guests over breakfast.

This topic was minor, when compared with their outrage, when it came to attempting to charter a boat. In the entrada of the hotel, James had left numerous leaflets from the several boat charter companies operating from Port de Sóller and also had details of other companies operating from other ports on the island. That morning, on the penultimate day of their stay, Harvey had come up to James after breakfast and asked him to arrange a boat charter for "him and the little lady" for that very day. James had pointed out that it might be difficult at such late notice but he would do his best. About half an hour and ten phone calls later, he realised that this was an impossibility, either for that day or for their last day as all boat charter companies' boats were completely booked up.

This was passed on to Harvey in the most polite and patient terms, but James' news was met by a lot of "God damn's" and "this wouldn't have happened if we'd gone to Martha's Vineyard". James soon realised that in his new chosen profession it was impossible to please all of the people all of the time.

He finished his shift just after lunchtime. Both boys were out for the afternoon with friends. Charlotte would be at the hotel until around six o'clock, so he felt it was a good time to go to his local gymnasium of Son Angelats in Sóller. James was doing his best to keep fit. He enjoyed food, and without the sometimes unpleasant necessity of burning calories, he knew he could quite easily start putting on the pounds. He tried to attend the gym several times per week, he played tennis once a week and played seven-a-side football at The University playing fields near Palma once a week with a group of both expat and Mallorcan guys. He had also recently purchased a road bike and bought himself all the accompanying Lycra gear and was beginning to get out on the roads once in a while. Today, more than most, he felt that doing a workout at the gym would be a good stress reliever.

He set off on his scooter from Fornalutx via the back streets of Sóller and rode along the main shopping street known as La Luna, which skirted the main Plaça d'Espanya in the centre of Sóller. He continued into Carrer de Bauçà, a narrow one-way street with extremely narrow footpaths, when, without warning, a man from his left-hand side stepped directly in front of him. He had no time to react but instinctively braked causing his tyres to screech, but a collision was unavoidable. James hit the man in the middle of the road from behind, causing the scooter to lurch to the right and with that, threw him from the vehicle. He landed with a thud onto the road with most of his weight landing on his right shoulder and then onto his head. He could feel the impact of his helmet hit the tarmac as he bounced at least once before coming to a halt. Dazed and confused and now with only one lens remaining in his prescription sunglasses, he slowly got to his feet. Several pedestrians in the street quickly gathered to offer assistance. James was shaken but apart from grazing his right shoulder and having a sore right kneecap, he was remarkably okay, considering that he was wearing his usual garb of shorts and T-shirt for going to the gym. He was more concerned about the pedestrian he had just collided with, irrespective of the reckless actions of the man, who had taken a large step into the middle of the road without looking behind him for oncoming traffic.

The man was lying prone on the ground on his front and it was only as the man was being helped up, that he noticed that his right leg was in a plaster cast. The man bent down and picked up a homemade-looking crutch, as James approached him.

"Are you alright? You didn't give me a chance. You just stepped right out in front of me," said James, as a passer-by handed him his missing lens from his sunglasses.

"Yeah, yeah, I'm okay. You must have been speeding or something," said the man, in a discernible Geordie accent.

"No mate, I wasn't speeding. You just stepped right out in front of me and I couldn't avoid hitting you. I think you should go to hospital to have your leg checked out. It seemed to take most of the impact. For all you know you could have broken it again," said James.

By now, there was a crowd of about twenty people around them and traffic was backed up to the plaça. Impatient drivers were now sounding their horns as the street was blocked by James' overturned scooter. Another bystander took it upon himself to pick up the moped and move it onto the narrow footpath to allow traffic to flow again. James had a cursory look at it from about twenty feet away and he was surprised to see the only visible damage appeared to be a broken rear light cluster, so he continued to speak to the man, who appeared to be in his mid-twenties. James could see a trickle of blood on the man's left shin.

"I think we need to swap details and contact the local police," said James, looking towards some of the on-lookers, who appeared to be mostly tourists, and asked for a pen and paper. A young girl approached him with a pen and a small jotter.

"Thank you," he said, as he accepted them and turned to the man again.

"What's your name mate?" he asked.

"Listen, I don't have time for this. I have a plane to catch to Newcastle in about three hours and I'm goin' to be late if we start all this. Look, I'm sorry. It was my fault. I'll pay you for any damage to your scooter but I need to go."

"Just a couple of details first. I don't want you suing me later for any injuries you may have sustained. What's your name?" asked James, with pen in hand.

"Look, oh for God's sake. My name's Baz, that's Barry Watkins. Give me that and I'll write down my mobile number."

The man, who was becoming impatient, grabbed the pen and pad and scribbled down a number. James took his mobile phone from the rucksack on his back and took a picture of the man while he was doing this and then took a photo of his moped. The man then handed the pen and pad back to James saying,

"Look, I don't need your details mate. I have to go or I'll miss my plane."

With that, he turned and hobbled off down the street in the direction of a car parked in Gran Via and James saw him get into the back of a white saloon vehicle, which then drove off. Baz, as he called himself, was obviously in a lot of pain from the way he was limping back to the car. James stood slightly flabbergasted and bemused by the man's attitude but put it down to him genuinely not wanting to miss his flight and perhaps realising that it was his own fault in the first instance.

The small cluster of people started to disperse and James ripped out the page with the details on it and handed the pad and the pen back to the young girl and thanked her. He was just starting to make his way back to his moped when someone tapped him on the back. James turned around to see a man holding out a brown wallet towards him.

"I think this is yours," said a man with a hint of a German accent.

James took it and examined it. It was a brown wallet, which, on looking inside, appeared to have quite a size-able wad of notes and he could also see a piece of paper, which he opened. It was an A4-size piece of paper which was a boarding card for a flight from Palma to Newcastle in the name of James Knox. It quickly became apparent that the wallet belonged to the guy who had called himself Baz.

"Thank you. I think it belongs to the other guy but I'll make sure he gets it back," said James with a smile.

The German stared at him and gave him a withering look as if to say, 'Yeah, sure you will' and went on his way.

James stood in a closed shop doorway as the street got back to normality, and further investigation inside the wallet produced a UK driving licence also in the name of James Knox. He concluded that the guy had given him a false name and most probably a dodgy mobile number but he tried ringing it anyway, in an effort to return Knox's wallet and boarding pass, without which, he may have difficulty in catching his flight. As expected the number was not recognised and failed to connect. James felt annoyed that the guy had lied but thought he now could have the last laugh, if he felt so inclined. However, he realised that Knox could probably still catch his flight by showing his passport and checking in at the check-in desk. Without his wallet, he may not have the means to pay for this service and judging by the thickness of the wallet, James estimated that there was over €1000 in notes in it.

He paused momentarily to consider his next course of action and placed the wallet in his rucksack. He rubbed his tender right shoulder and removed his crash helmet to get a better look at the state of his injuries. He looked at his hand after wiping his shoulder and could see that the wound was already starting to congeal but it was not that serious. His right knee had some swelling and was sore to touch but would just need to be cleaned with some anti-septic. He had, by all accounts, been quite lucky. He placed the lens back into his sunglasses and placed them on his head, whilst walking across the street to his moped, after checking for traffic from behind him.

"The stupid arse," he murmured under his breath. James felt fine to get back on his moped but had ruled out going to the gym after what had just happened. Despite his annoyance at the attitude of Knox, he felt he could not knowingly hang onto the guy's wallet and cash and momentarily considered riding to the airport in Palma to return it to him, as he had time to get there before the Newcastle flight took off. His car was in for its annual service in Fornalutx but even if was ready it might be a bit too tight for time, to ride back there and pick up his car. James considered his options. *No,* he thought, *I'm not riding my 125cc scooter on the motorway for a guy who has lied to me.*

James, in the three years of owning his scooter had never ridden it on the motorway, as he felt it wasn't powerful enough to produce the speeds needed not to become a hazard. He then thought he should just hand the wallet in to the local police station and let them deal with the hassle of returning it, but it wasn't in his character to just take the easy way out, so he decided to

ring Ramon, to see if the local police would be prepared
to take it, there and then, to Palma Airport to restore it
to Knox before his flight left.

"Hola. Dígame," said Ramon.

"It's just a long shot Ramon but I don't suppose you
would ask the local police here in Sóller if they would do
a run to Palma Airport, to return a wallet and boarding
pass to a muppet who has just made me crash into him
while he was on foot in Sóller, about ten minutes ago?"
asked James.

"I could ask my friend, Miquel Busquets, who's in
the Guardia Civil in Sóller to do it if you like? Where
are you at the minute?" asked Ramon.

"I'm close to Gran Via, in Sóller, holding this guy's
wallet. His flight leaves in about two and a half hours
back to the UK, and there must be about €1000 in it,"
replied James.

"I tell you what. I am only in Palmanyola, at my old
neighbour's house, having a coffee. I am going back to
Palma anyway, so why don't I meet you on this side of
the tunnel and I, or we, can take it to the guy ourselves?"

"Are you sure you don't mind? I don't know if the
guy deserves this to be honest, but I don't like loose
ends and I wouldn't mind seeing his face when I hand it
over after he has lied to me. Okay, I'll see you there in
a few minutes on my scooter. Chao."

James made his way to their meeting point on the
other side of the Sóller tunnel and parked on the opposite side of the road and waited for Ramon. A few
minutes later, Ramon pulled up alongside him and
wound down his window.

"Do you want me to take it to him or do you want to
come too?" he asked.

"If it's alright with you, I'll come too," said James, already half in the front passenger seat.

He placed his crash helmet and rucksack on the back seat of the car and put on his seatbelt before turning to Ramon and saying,

"What a day I'm having! First I get abuse from this old American pain in the arse because all the boat charters are booked and then this 'culo' steps right out in front of me and I go arse over tit on my scooter, and then he has the gall to lie to me, so he'd better be grateful for this, I can tell you. Oh yeah, and his leg is in plaster," said James, shaking his head with incredulity.

"Do you know his name…although as you say his leg is in plaster so I can ring ahead and get the Guardia Civil to look for him, to let him know his wallet has been found and is on its way."

"His real name is James Knox, although he told me some other bollocks at the time. He's about twenty-five, short dark hair, wearing a blue T-shirt and white shorts but there can't be too many people arriving at Palma Airport with their right leg in plaster, and he's due out on the 3.30pm flight to Newcastle, England," said James.

Ramon operated his mobile phone via his in-car Bluetooth system and James could hear him relay all the information he had given him to the Guardia Civil at the airport. The two men chatted for the remainder of the short journey and Ramon parked in the drop-off zone where both men alighted from the car swiftly and entered the airport. Almost immediately inside, Ramon's mobile phone rang and he stopped in his tracks after a few seconds of conversation and looked at James with an exasperated expression and then he ended the call. Turning to James he said,

"Okay. Two officers saw this guy Knox with a crutch and started to walk over to him to tell him we were coming with his wallet and they say that when they asked him was he James Knox, he threw his crutch at them and started to try and run away. Now obviously he didn't get very far on one good leg, so the officers have detained him and they have him in a police office, just along here," said Ramon, pointing behind James.

"Really? That's a bit weird. Do you think he thought it was because of the accident and he just panicked?" asked James.

He pulled out the wallet from his rucksack and looked at the contents more closely. There was a small pocket for coins, which he opened and emptied the contents into his hand. There were several coins and also a small piece of a brown substance, which both men instantly recognised as cannabis resin.

"This is making a bit more sense now. I don't think he knows he has lost his wallet and he thought they were going to find this 'blow' on him and he's had it on his toes. This might be more fun than I thought. Am I still allowed to speak to him?" asked James.

"Let's see what he has to say for himself and yes, you are a witness and simply returning his property," said Ramon.

James followed Ramon along the concourse to an unmarked door. Ramon opened it and walked inside, followed by James. There were two uniformed, armed Guardia Civil officers standing inside and seated at a table was the man whom James had collided with earlier in Sóller, who he now knew to be called James Knox. Ramon greeted the officers and one of them recounted to Ramon that they had approached the man to inform him that his wallet had been found and he had only got as far as asking his name, when without warning, the man threw his makeshift crutch at the officers and limped off as quickly as he could, away from the airport terminal. The officers shouted at him to stop and then gave chase and caught him only a short distance away. The Guardia Civil officer couldn't stop himself from laughing at the lunacy of the man, considering his right leg was in plaster.

Ramon then turned to Knox.

"I am Comisario Ramon Martinez. I am a police officer. You have already met my friend here, James Gordon, I understand. Can you tell me your name please?" asked Ramon, sitting down opposite Knox at the table. James then sat down beside Ramon.

"Look, what is this about? I am going to miss my flight back home if you keep me here much longer and my leg hurts, no thanks to your mate here," he said, nodding his head towards James.

"You haven't answered my question. What is your name?" said Ramon firmly.

"Alright. Is this because I give your mate moody details? This is fuckin' unbelievable," said Knox, in an agitated manner. "My name is Jimmy Knox. Okay? Can I go now please?"

"I think you might be missing something," said Ramon.

"Like what?" Knox asked, frowning.

"Like this maybe?" said James as he placed the wallet on the table.

Knox looked at it and he exhaled with an audible sigh of relief but this was quickly replaced with a look akin to that of a rabbit caught in headlights.

"You have got my wallet? I didn't know I had lost it. Is that why I'm here?" he stammered.

"My friend here has told me how you had caused him to come off his scooter and doing the sensible thing has asked you for your name and telephone number. He was concerned for your well-being. You have told him lies. Why would you do this? Despite this, he has recovered your wallet with a lot of money inside and the boarding card for your flight home. Knowing you had lied to him, he could be forgiven for thinking, 'Fuck this guy. I am going to keep this money. This guy has damaged my scooter and my shoulder hurts.' I could understand it if that was his attitude but it wasn't. No, he calls me to see if I can help get it to you before you attempt to fly back to England and I said, 'Sure, James, I will help you to help this guy.' So that, my friend, was why we were coming here: to help you," said Ramon, staring intently at Knox, who appeared to be embarrassed and he diverted his gaze to the floor, before lifting it and saying,

"Sorry, I'm sorry. Hey, thanks for doing this mate and I'm sorry for what happened before. It's been a bad week for me," he said, tapping the plaster cast on his leg.

"So what happened?" asked James.

"Oh shit, you know, too much drink and then I fell; yeah I fell from my balcony."

"Where were you staying?" asked Ramon.

"Oh man, what's with all the questions? Look I appreciate you returning my wallet and all but can I please go now?"

"Which hospital did you attend and why did they not give you a proper crutch?" asked Ramon directly.

"I don't know man. I was out of it," he said, giving James a look appealing for him to help the situation.

"Don't look at me. I have no jurisdiction here. It is this man's questions you need to answer and I'm sure you will be on your way. But I do have one question. Why did you throw your crutch at the officers here and then run or at least hop off?" asked James, trying to keep a straight face.

Knox squirmed in his chair, looking towards the floor, clearly trying to find an answer but unable to provide one.

"Before you say it was because of the little bit of blow in your wallet, I'm sure you realise that it is legal in Spain to have this amount of cannabis for personal use in your home and it is not a major crime if you are in a public place but rather you can get a small fine. No, I think it is something else and I certainly don't think for a minute you thought you were being stopped for giving me a dodgy name and phone number. So, go on Jimmy, tell us why you ran?" asked James, beginning to get an uncomfortable feeling in his gut.

"I'm not saying anything more. Have I been arrested?" Knox asked.

Ramon was giving him a steely look and James could tell that he was also 'smelling the same rat' as him. Ramon then spoke to the Guardia Civil officers and one left the room.

"Because you had this drug in your possession, I am going to search you for more drugs that may not be just for your own use," said Ramon, standing up. The remaining Guardia Civil officer approached Knox and motioned for him to stand up.

"This is fuckin' unbelievable! You had better explain to my missus why I'm not comin' back home and to my boss why I won't be at work tomorrow, like!" said Knox, with a more pronounced Geordie accent, clearly getting angry.

The Guardia Civil officer started to conduct a drug search and asked Knox to empty his pockets, remove his one shoe and sock and then to take off his T-shirt and pull down his shorts. Nothing was found. The officer then produced a pair of disposable surgical gloves from his pocket and spoke to Ramon in Spanish, which James assumed was him asking Ramon if a more thorough search was required. Ramon shook his head and replied that he would wait for the drugs dog. Right on cue, the other Guardia Civil officer returned with another officer and a lively looking German Shepherd. The dog was barking loudly at Knox.

"Fuckin' hell, get that thing away from me!" he shouted.

His handler took the dog off its leash. The dog showed some interest in the wallet by lying down and staying very still and quiet, before moving close to it on the table. His handler then removed the cannabis from the wallet and handed it to Ramon, who nodded. The officer then bounced a tennis ball on the floor and the dog quickly grabbed it and was praised by his handler. The officer then took the ball off his dog and ushered him to search further. Immediately, the dog zoomed in on Knox's right leg in the cast and stood perfectly still within a few inches of the cast, which was clearly making Knox uneasy.

The officer once again bounced the tennis ball and praised the dog and confirmed to Ramon that the dog had sniffed drugs in his cast and because of the dog's trained standing still response the officer said it was cocaine.

"Okay, my friend. Here is the situation you find yourself in. This expertly trained dog is telling me that you have clearly got cocaine inside your plaster cast on your leg and I am guessing there is a lot down there, so I am giving these officers authority to remove it from your leg to find what is down there. Once we find it, I am going to charge you with the most serious drug offence of my choice, after which, you will go to court and then to a Spanish prison for a very long time. A pretty boy like you won't last too long in one of our jails. Now, is there anything you want to tell me?" said Ramon, without taking a breath.

James hadn't seen this persona from Ramon since his first meeting with him in the police station in Sóller. James was impressed with Ramon's monologue and actually a little frightened for Knox, despite knowing Ramon to be a very fair and personable man both on and off duty.

Knox sank back down into his seat and put his head in his hands, as if admitting defeat, only looking up to point and shout,

"Move that fuckin' dog away from me, will you? I'll tell you what you want to know. I'm fucked anyway."

Chapter 4

Between a Rock and a Hard Place

A couple of months previously, the commentary from the last race of the day at Sunderland Greyhound Stadium reached fever pitch. Jimmy watched nervously, as his dog, out of trap 5, wearing a yellow jacket and optimistically called Northern Flyer, at odds of 4-1, was still in the race until the final bend. It was a close second right up until the line but failed to make up the ground to win. Jimmy screwed up his betting slip and threw it on the ground with all the other beaten dockets. A sense of hopelessness and foreboding consumed him. He had just lost £500 over the course of the evening. He wasn't there to enjoy a night at the races with good company, a few drinks and a casual flutter. Jimmy was there as he had a gambling addiction and it was due to his addiction that he felt sick to the pit of his stomach. The £500 that he had staked was his last chance to accrue the money he needed to pay back his long overdue interest on a small loan he had taken out from a notorious Sunderland loan shark.

Jimmy's life was very much a hand-to-mouth existence. He had left school without any qualifications to
speak of and had spent many years playing the benefits
system for all it was worth. He had managed to get a
job in a warehouse as a 'humper and dumper' and went
on to get his fork-lift truck driving test and was quite
happy for a while. He had got his then girlfriend,
Simone, pregnant but Jimmy wanted to do the right
thing by her so they moved in together and three years
had passed since Simone gave birth to their daughter,
Raquel. Jimmy was only twenty-five years old but he
hadn't worked for over two years, since he sustained
crush injuries to one of his hands, while messing about on
the forklift truck at work. He was in receipt of invalidity
benefit but he had got himself into a self-deprecating
spiral, with not being motivated to find another job and
starting to gamble out of boredom.

The gambling became more severe as time went on,
and what started as small accumulator bets, where he
had a modicum of success, soon turned into larger bets
to try and relive the thrill of the wins he had achieved.
His gambling was affecting his mood and his personality.
His relationships changed beyond recognition with
Simone and his daughter. The little money he had from
his benefits, which was needed to put food on the table
and clothe his family, was too much of a temptation for
him and over the last few weeks he had been going to
the race track in an effort to try and recoup some of the
things he had pawned to feed his gambling addiction.

It had got so bad that he had taken Simone's engagement ring from the top of her bedside cabinet after she
had taken it off to have a bath. He had saved for months
to buy the ring in the first place and hoped one day to

be able to give her a wedding she would be proud of. He then had to lie to her about knowing where it had gone but she had a fair idea that it was his gambling addiction that was responsible and holding the whole family to ransom.

Jimmy was disgusted by his own actions. He thought, if he could just get a run of luck he could get the ring out of hock and treat his family to a weekend away at the seaside and restore some self-respect, even for a short time. He knew of a loan shark, who had a reputation for lending to pretty much anyone. He knew the reason for this was that the few people he had heard about, who had not paid him back on time or tried to avoid repayment, had anything of value taken from their homes by his henchmen and were badly beaten. Tony Mason was a name that struck fear into the working-class people of Sunderland and with good reason.

Despite knowing the risks, Jimmy persevered anyway with his course of action and called round to a house on the Pennywell Estate, where he knew that Mason operated from. He knew that loan sharking was not the only string to his bow and even the dogs in the street knew that he operated Sunderland's main illicit drugs trade, although Mason had not got his hands dirty more recently, after serving a five-year stretch at Her Majesty's pleasure for drug importation. He had an army of dealers and enforcers to do his dirty work for him but his reputation for brutality was well-founded.

Jimmy managed to borrow £500 with an interest rate of 20% per week and he was to repay the debt in full within one month, if not before. That meant that if he waited a month to repay the loan, he would owe over £1000. He accepted the terms and was made to understand the risks. Tony Mason himself had pointed out the consequences to him personally so it was clear what his obligations were. Jimmy had genuinely intended to go to Ramsden's Pawnbrokers and reclaim Simone's engagement ring, and with the remaining £200 he would go to the Friday night racing at the greyhound track in an effort to win enough money to repay the loan early and perhaps have enough winnings to take Simone and Raquel to Whitley Bay on the coast for a day or two. However, he convinced himself that he might need all the money for his bets, in case 'lady luck' didn't shine on him from the outset.

Things didn't go exactly to plan for Jimmy that first night but he managed to walk away with just over £250 of his £500 loan. Over the coming days and weeks, he continued to attend the greyhound track and he topped up his stake with his meagre invalidity benefit, meaning once again, his family would not have enough to make ends meet. His month's grace with Tony Mason was up and he had already been approached by Mason's henchmen on the way to the track but he had managed to convince them that he would have all the money by the end of the night. He had gone to the race meet with £500, knowing that he would need to double it, just to pay Mason back, never mind getting Simone's ring back or having money for food. The weekend away he realised was pie in the sky.

The first six races on the card had been a mixed bag and by the last race he had about £300 left to stake. Taking this into account, and despite feeling that the form of the favourite dog looked like a sure thing, he realised he needed to take a punt on the 4-1 outsider, Northern Flyer, and to put it all 'on the nose' for him to win. As his dog was narrowly beaten into second place, the gravity of his situation hit home and Jimmy felt sick. He cursed himself and his affliction and began to worry about what lay in store for him. He knew that a time extension was not on the cards. He considered doing a robbery at his local off-license but he knew it was protected with various anti-robbery devices, like CCTV, a central station alarm directly to the police station and the counter was behind a cage. He then thought about disappearing for a few days but he knew that Mason's men would call at his house and he feared for Simone and his daughter.

He left the stadium and walked aimlessly around the city and down by the banks of the River Wear. He realised that it was his addiction that was bringing a lot of unhappiness to his family and considered throwing himself into the dark, murky water and ending it all but he couldn't bring himself to do it. He loved Simone and he wanted a better life for his daughter than growing up with just her mother struggling to cope. *No*, he thought, *that is the coward's way out. I am responsible for getting us into this shit and I need to get us out of it.*

He resolved that he needed to go straight back to the house on the Pennywell Estate and own up to not being able to repay the loan. *What's the worst thing that can happen?* he thought, as his mind raced and he remembered some of the stories his mates down his local pub recounted; of various people having crossed Tony Mason and who had either disappeared or were going to require a wheelchair for the rest of their lives. Jimmy stopped momentarily and put his hands on his knees and took several deep breaths. He could have cried but he knew it wouldn't help the situation.

"Fuckin' man up and grow a pair," he said to himself. He waited for a few seconds, bit his nails and looked all around him, becoming more and more paranoid that Mason's thugs would turn up at any minute before he could have any potential credence, that he was on his way, of his own volition to face the music.

He started walking again in the direction of the Pennywell Estate and it was now nearly midnight. He didn't know if Mason would even be available for him to attempt to appeal to a better nature that Jimmy knew he didn't have, and that it was more likely that Mason's thugs would dish him out a severe beating and tell him the debt would be doubled, or something to that effect.

As he approached the house, Jimmy could hear the sound of heavy base music emanating from within. He tentatively knocked on the door. There was no reply and he considered walking away but he stood his ground and he knocked firmly and loudly and continued to knock until he heard the sound of the reinforced cage door, behind the front door, being opened. The front door then opened and one of Mason's men was standing there with a bottle of beer in his hand.

"What the fook do you want?" he said, snarling aggressively at Jimmy.

"I, I'm here to see Tony," stammered Jimmy.

"Well, he's no fookin' here, so you can fook right oot of it before I fookin' glass you man!" shouted the stocky man, pushing Jimmy backwards away from the door as he got ready to close it.

The man looked slightly familiar to Jimmy and although he risked the wrath of him further, Jimmy asked,

"Mickey? Mickey Finn, is that you?"

The man had already partially closed the door but opened it up and walked closer to Jimmy, looking him up and down before bursting to life, smiling and saying,

"Little Jimmy Knox! You little bastard, is that you? I haven't seen you since school days man! What are you looking for Tony for, man? You don't wanna get on the wrong side a Tony man."

"Jesus, Mickey you've changed. I hardly recognised you man. You've fairly bulked up since school," started Jimmy.

"Aye man, that'll be the steroids and me pumpin' iron and that. You kna when we used to get picked on at school and that. Well, I thought, I'm not havin' that no more, so I bulked up and I've been workin' for Tony for a while like."

"Listen, Mickey, I'm in the shit. I owe Tony money from a loan and tonight's my last night to pay. What should I do? I haven't got the money to pay him right now but I will pay it back, I swear on my daughter's life, I will pay it back."

"Oh Jesus Jimmy, you are puttin' me in a fookin' awkward position here. I usually have to sort out the bastards that don't pay Tony, otherwise I fookin' get it in the neck. Do you kna what I mean like?" said Mickey, getting agitated.

"Look I tell you what I will do for you. Tony is droppin' by in aboot half an hour and he was askin' me did I kna anyone who could do a little job for him overseas like. It was gonna pay quite well mind but it had to be somebody without a criminal record. Do you have a criminal record Jimmy?" he asked.

Jimmy thought for a moment. He had been cautioned as a juvenile for a minor offence but had never been to court or convicted of an offence.

"No, Mickey. I'm clean as a whistle, me like," he replied.

"Well look, I'll ring Tony now and vouch for you and maybe we can work summit out. You wait outside like 'cos Tony won't let anybody but his lads inside here after ten, unless it's to give someone a hidin' like," said Mickey, with no sign of a smirk, so Jimmy took it that he wasn't joking and swallowed hard.

The door closed and he could hear the cage inside being locked and the music was then turned down. Jimmy sat by the kerbside and waited.

It was almost one o'clock before a black Porsche Cayenne with tinted windows pulled up close to where Jimmy was sitting. Three large men got out and started to walk towards him. Tony Mason was one of them. All three men stood around him, towering over him and he felt very intimidated. Jimmy stood up, almost falling over a kerbstone in doing so.

"Have you got my fuckin' money?" asked Mason.

"Mr Mason, I was just talking to Mickey Finn and telling him I need more time. Did he not phone you?" asked Jimmy.

"I'm the one askin' the fuckin' questions here. Have you or have you not got my fuckin' money?" barked Mason, into Jimmy's face.

"No sir, I…" was all Jimmy got to say, before he saw Mason nod to one of his men, who punched Jimmy full in the abdomen, sending him reeling to the ground in pain.

The great force of the single punch had winded him badly and he was sucking in air in an attempt to get his breath back. He was now on all fours, holding his ribcage. He had been sucker punched and was unable to defend himself. *If they continue with the assault I won't be able to fight back*, he thought. After what seemed like an eternity, Jimmy managed to get his breath back but he remained on the ground, holding his tender abdomen and side. All three men had stood over him the whole time but remained silent.

"Now do I have your attention?" asked Mason, in a slow, deliberate manner.

"Yes, Mr Mason," said Jimmy, timidly, looking up at him.

"I lend you money, my own fuckin' money that I work hard to earn. I tell you the terms by which that loan has to be repaid. You agree to those terms. I need to make some money on the deal because I am a business-man. I'm not a fuckin' charity to be taken advantage of by cunts like you. This is business and if you don't play by the rules, there are consequences and I told you what those consequences were but yet here we are, standing in the fuckin' street in the middle of the night, when I should be at home shaggin' my bird, but I'm here dealing with you, you little shit," said Mason, before kicking Jimmy in the midriff almost in the same tender spot where the punch connected, causing him acute pain. He curled up into a ball in agony and expected a further onslaught of blows to reign in on him.

To his surprise and relief, no more came but he remained in agony and on edge, expecting more violence against him at any moment.

"Now, you may have heard rumours about me. I know the rumours and for the most part I would say they are all true, except for one that was circulating about me cutting Fat Phil's knob off. I had nothing to do with that. The fact that he has only got seven toes, I may have had a hand in that. The point I am trying to make here Jimmy is that it is time to pay the piper. Now, you say you can't pay me and so I can send the boys here round to your gaff and take what's rightfully mine but I know for a fact that you, you little bastard, have fuck all worth takin' in your shithole because little Jimmy here has got a serious fuckin' gamblin' problem. His problem is that he can't stop losing.

"I could go round and have my way with your missus but that would only knock a fiver off the debt, from what I know of her, so I can see only two options left. Option one: I get the boys here to do a bit of DIY surgery inside and remove, say a kidney or your spleen and I try to sell it to some dodgy spare body parts company, or option two: you do a job for me and I might just let you live. So what's it to be? You're a gamblin' man: one or two?" asked Mason.

Jimmy had no realistic choice other than to go for option two, whatever that entailed. He realised that whatever it was, it would be at some considerable risk to him otherwise Mason would not ask someone like him to do it.

"Option two, Mr Mason," he said.

"Right boys. Bring our new associate inside so we can discuss his little job," said Mason.

His two minders picked Jimmy up by his arms to his feet and ushered him towards the door of the house. The cage door creaked and the front door was opened by Mickey and all four men went inside. Jimmy followed Mason into a makeshift living room with grubby sofas and which was dimly lit. It had bars on the window and a coffee table littered with empty beer cans and bottles and several overflowing ashtrays. The air was thick with a combination of cannabis and cigarette smoke and stale body odour.

"Fuckin' open that window Mickey, it fuckin' stinks in 'ere and clean that shit up, will ya?" shouted Mason.

"Sorry, Tony. I'll do it right away," said Mickey, jumping to it.

Mason sat down on a sofa and motioned for Jimmy to sit down opposite him.

"I suppose you want a fuckin' beer then?" he said.

"No. I'm alright, but thanks anyway," added Jimmy quickly.

"Of course you want a beer. I want a beer. Mickey! Two beers!" he ordered.

Mickey brought in two cold beers and took one to Mason, before handing one to Jimmy and giving him a sly wink, as if to say things were going to be alright.

Jimmy took a small sip of his beer but was watching Mason the whole time and occasionally had a cursory glance round towards his two minders who were both standing just inside the doorway.

"Mickey, you can stay for this too," said Mason.

"Okay boss," said Mickey and he sat down on the arm of Jimmy's sofa.

"Mickey tells me you and he were at school together."

"That's right. Silverdale Comprehensive on Buckthorn Lane."

"Mickey says he can vouch for you and he says you've never been in bother with the law. Is that right Jimmy?" asked Mason, staring intently at Jimmy, before taking a swig from his beer bottle.

"No, I've never been in trouble with the police like," he replied.

"The thing is Jimmy, I have a very important job for you and it involves you getting on a plane tomorrow afternoon and goin' to Majorca. Now, it's no fuckin' holiday mind. I need you to be focused. Have you got a passport, Jimmy?"

"Aye. I have."

"Well here's what's gonna happen. You drink your beer and my boys here will drive you home. I want you to be back here for no later than ten o'clock tomorrow morning with an overnight bag and your passport. I have already booked a seat on the flight from Newcastle and I will change it into your name tomorrow. You will be away for a couple of days, so make sure you make up a story for 'hinny'. Under no circumstances are you to tell her where you are going or what you are doing. Do you understand Jimmy?" asked Mason firmly.

"Yes, yes I understand."

"Now, you are to bring something back for me and I will give you all the details when I see you tomorrow and if everything goes as I expect it to Jimmy, then your debt will be fully paid. Now fuck off," said Mason, necking the remainder of his bottle of beer.

Jimmy stood up and set his still half full beer bottle on the coffee table. His stomach was still hurting. He walked towards the doorway where Mason's minders were waiting for him but Jimmy turned and said to Mason,

"There's just one thing Mr Mason," he started.

"Go on then, let's hear it," responded Mason, gesturing for Mickey to get him another beer.

Jimmy paused and contemplated saying 'forget it', but he saw an opportunity and he said,

"I have absolutely no money to my name. I lost it all on the dogs tonight trying to get your money for you."

"My fuckin' heart is bleedin' for you. Mickey! Bring me a box of tissues as well as that beer, he's gonna have me greetin' in a minute. Go on, spit it oot man!"

"The thing is, I will need some money for food and stuff and I don't know yet what exactly it is you want me to bring back but I'm guessing that if I'm caught with whatever it is you will want me to be quiet…"

Mason stood up and looked angry.

Jimmy quickly followed it up with, "No, no. That's not what I meant to say. I would never grass on you and I didn't mean it to sound as if I was disrespecting you… it's just, a man needs some money in his pockets and I don't want to have to borrow more money from you but I need to get me girl's engagement ring from the pawnbrokers like. That's all I meant," said Jimmy, looking for any favourable sign in Mason's demeanour.

"The kid's got a lotta bottle makin' demands like that, eh Mickey? I tell ya what Jimmy, let me think on it and I'll give ya my answer in the morning and Jimmy, divvin' na be late mind."

With that, Jimmy walked out of the house and got into the back seat of the Porsche and was dropped off outside his flat. He walked up to the communal entrance hall and stepped inside. He sighed with relief that he was still alive but with the realisation of what he had got himself involved in he didn't want to think about it right at that moment. It was nearly two o'clock in the morning and he had to be back at the Pennywell Estate in eight hours. The lies he was going to have to concoct for Simone's benefit he would work out in the morning. He was in with the big boys now and his primary goal was survival.

Chapter 5

The King is Dead,
Long Live the King!

The morning alarm was barely audible when it first went off but gradually it increased in volume to the point where ignoring it any longer was not an option. Mason rolled over and hit the snooze button, only to go through the same procedure ten minutes later, this time switching it off on his mobile phone on top of his bedside cabinet. He sat up, yawned and stretched and put both feet on the floor as a pre-curser to standing up but checked his WhatsApp messages on his mobile and then proceeded to do the same on his work mobile. There was nothing that needed his immediate attention from overnight, so he stood up and sauntered into his en suite bathroom and emptied his bladder, whilst continuing to yawn and stretch, being careful not to hit the rim of the toilet seat, which he had left down. On finishing, he stood in front of his well-lit vanity mirror over his wash hand basin and checked out his muscular physique, tensing his muscles and posing as if he was in a body- building competition. Satisfied with what he saw, he brushed his teeth and then took a hot shower.

Tony Mason was born and bred in the Hendon area of inner city Sunderland. He was the youngest of five children, having two older brothers and two older sisters, and throughout his early years had a relatively happy, normal childhood. He lived in a deprived area, in a three-bedroomed council house and had always shared a bedroom with his two older brothers but there was always enough food on the table and although money was tight, he considered his house a happy home. He had tried his best at school but was not gifted academically nor was he particularly interested in or good at sport, unlike one of his older brothers, Gary, who was deemed good enough to be signed up by Sunderland Football Club at the age of sixteen. This was a big thing for the Mason family and for the whole area; that a working class lad might potentially play for a Premiership football team and even better because it was for their beloved 'Black Cats'.

As Gary's career progressed and he made it into Sunderland's reserve team, his wages increased significantly and so too did the respect he gained from local friends and neighbours. Tony was initially very proud of his older brother, but after dropping out of school with minimal qualifications, Tony struggled to find any meaningful employment. Although his brother was supplementing his family's income and Tony was directly benefitting from this, Tony was becoming jealous of his brother's success.

Having little else to do with his time, he started doing minor errand jobs for some of the older boys on his estate. At that time, illegal drugs were rife on his estate, as they were in most estates, but he had no interest in them. He looked up to a couple of older guys who were heavily into body building, who trained at the local gymnasium-*cum*-boxing club on the edge of his estate. Tony would hang around with a couple of mates and earn a few quid by delivering batches of needles and steroids to some clients of the bodybuilders at the gym. He didn't feel like he was doing anything wrong and he saw the respect these guys gained just by being 'ripped'.

Tony was taken under the wing of one of these guys, known as 'Spider', due to the spider's web tattoo he had on his neck. Soon, Tony was attending the gym on a daily basis to work out, and seeing the results that steroids were having on his mentors' physiques, he soon followed in their footsteps and started to see quick results. Tony, now eighteen, had transformed himself from a scrawny, eleven stone seventeen-year-old with low self-esteem, into a well-defined, muscular, sixteen stone, arrogant kid who was now dealing in steroids himself and making a fair living from it.

As time went on, he was introduced to other body builders, who dealt not only in steroids but in other, even more lucrative, illicit drugs and he saw the lifestyle these men had and he wanted a piece of it too. For him, his mind was already made up but what reinforced it for him, was when he saw the decline of his brother Gary after he was released by Sunderland Football Club, when he sustained serious multiple fractures to his leg whilst on holiday with a group of his friends. After several operations and steel pins being inserted, Gary's playing days as a professional footballer were over all too soon and with it the admiration of the local community. Having no other prospects, his brother fell into bouts of depression and drug misuse, culminating in his premature death from a heroin overdose, aged just twenty-three.

Tony realised just how fleeting and fickle success was within any field but he was resolute he would not allow it to happen to him and he had to succeed, no matter what the cost. Success for him was measured by what trainers you wore, the car you drove, what your girl-friend looked like, and whether you were respected or feared by your contemporary group. He had started to amass the trappings but for him he had only just started.

He had become involved with a criminal gang based in Sunderland and had now moved out of the parental home. He still attended the gym seven days a week and was still heavily dependent on steroids. Whether he had become a different person gradually or whether the steroids were responsible solely for his moods swings, he didn't know or care, but he soon became feared by dealers and users alike for his lack of patience and for his ruthlessness and brutality when it came to violence.

He would justify his actions with the phrase, 'big boys' games, big boys' rules', and soon he was not satis-fied with his slice of the pie that he had been given up to that point. This burning ambition culminated in him making a pact with a rival drug gang in neighbouring Newcastle and he then dispatched his own drug gang boss in a manner that no-one would ever find the body or initiate a murder inquiry. With this major hurdle being overcome, Mason's career path to success and seniority within the north-east's drug trade grew rapidly and soon he was involved in sizeable imported shipments of both cocaine and heroin.

His involvement in this lucrative enterprise was temporarily suspended when he got too personally involved with a large shipment of cocaine. It arrived at Newcastle docks, only to have been first intercepted by Interpol and then passed to the National Crime Agency, who allowed the cargo to be offloaded but covertly followed its transportation to a warehouse in Sunderland, where armed police and other agencies were waiting to apprehend the offenders. Mason was one of them, as yet unable or unwilling to delegate the overseeing of the landing and distribution of such a large haul.

He spent the next five years in HM Prison Durham for drug importation offences but he still ran his business from his prison cell over that period. It made his resolve all the greater to succeed and made his trust in people even less, although he did have time to realise that he must never again leave a trail of evidence to him. He thought that it might be practical for him to consider one major deal and then to live off the rewards of that and to reinvest it into legitimate, legal businesses. His stretch in prison was like him going to university. He would spend much of his time listening to other inmates' stories of how the various law enforcement agencies operated and how his fellow inmates would bring in large shipments of drugs undetected. Mason was like a sponge, soaking it all up and mentally making notes of all the most relevant bits for his proposed 'mega job', once he got out. He was proactive in befriending other inmates with clout and once out, he was able to foster further contacts with some heavy hitters in the field of European drug importation and distribution.

Mason was no mug. After his incarceration, he realised the fewer individuals who were involved in an operation, the greater the chance of success, but he had also come to the conclusion that, in order to get a payday big enough for him to retire from the arena, he had to involve others with more capital than he had. He had certainly done well for himself financially over the previous ten years. The first thing he did when he was released from Durham Prison, almost as a 'two fingers up' to the system and to the Governor of Durham Prison, was to buy a Grade II listed, large, period Georgian townhouse, overlooking the cricket pitch in the centre of Durham for in excess of £1.5 million. He spent the next two weeks kitting it out with a state-of-the-art security system and a fully-equipped gymnasium, much to the disgust of the governor, who now had Mason as a close neighbour.

Mason started sending only his most trusted lieutenants to meetings throughout Europe, to garner support for a potentially huge payday for all those concerned. He started working with some of his European counterparts as a show of good faith and when he felt the time was right he arranged financing for a major shipment of cocaine. He had observed that in recent years, international drug enforcement agencies tended to pay more interest to shipments coming from Brazil and Venezuela, reflecting the increasing production of cocaine from countries like Bolivia and Peru.

He was also aware that a lot of focus was on transit areas like the Caribbean, where onward transportation of the illegal drugs would tend to go to Rotterdam, Antwerp or Valencia, so Mason wanted to do something different. His plan was to send a shipment directly from a previously notorious but now second-tier country in cocaine production: Columbia, and bring his cargo to Europe, not through one of the large ports but via an island port, Palma de Mallorca and then onward to the port of Marseilles in France.

He had spent some time in prison with an inmate who spent a lot of his time making models and using dyes and resins. Mason had seen first-hand the result of him making very realistic wooden branches from plaster of Paris, a resin and a brown dye. So he came up with an idea of using this methodology to potentially get his large shipment into Europe undetected. What he needed was a 'cook' both in Columbia and in Palma.

He had already changed the route of his supply to the UK. During his time in prison, he had gained the trust of a major cartel that was linked to FARC rebels and from whom he had been buying cocaine in relatively significant quantities over the previous five years. He knew the Columbians had corrupt officials at Cartagena port in their pockets and a 'rip on' team, who were able to get the drugs into containers at the port and replace the security seals with duplicates.

He had dispatched one of his lieutenants to Palma, Mallorca, to set up a legitimate-looking import business, and he had acquired the lease on a warehouse at Palma docks. Mason had also learned a great deal about money laundering and setting up fake business accounts in offshore havens, thanks to his education at Durham, and within days of his release he had arranged for the creation of numerous 'shell companies' in various tax havens throughout the world.

He had been sent a small test sample of the product in its changed form, courtesy of the Columbian cook, having dissolved the cocaine with solvent and glue and then placed it in a mould with a dye. It had simply been placed in a 'Jiffy bag' and sent through the post, disguised as a medal. He had then got another cook to reverse the process and re-dissolve the medal and extract the cocaine, as a dry run to the larger operation, and he was impressed with the purity of the product.

As a 'belt and braces' measure, he had decided that the UK-based cook should go to Mallorca and break down the product when it arrived at the warehouse at Palma. The product was to be in pallets and also disguised as charcoal pieces in bags and was to be sent by container to his newly created 'charcoal imports business'. The pallets would be made from a mixture containing cocaine and dyed in moulds to look like authentic wooden pallets. Real charcoal would be mixed with some further disguised product in case of inspection and to help throw drug dogs off the scent.

However, Mason was not content with this on its own. Not satisfied by bringing it into Europe via an island port – which would be unusual for a large Continental European-bound drug shipment – and then sending it onwards in its disguised state, he added another layer to the subterfuge. He decided to set up a 'cook's lab' completely away from prying eyes, and one of his shell companies had purchased a small and basic mountain property, known as an 'olivar'. It was not overlooked and had vehicular access and electricity and was in the Tramuntana Mountains on the western side of Mallorca. The house, which was surrounded by olive trees, came also with around three acres of orange trees. Mason had read that oranges from this part of Mallorca, known as The Sóller Valley, had been exported to France, mostly through Marseilles, for over a hundred years.

He saw an opportunity to help cause confusion and help to mix up the modus operandi, so he arranged for his second Mallorca-based company to be legitimately set up as an orange export business. The UK cook was now in residence in the olivar and his equipment was operational there. The oranges would be picked and the insides would be sucked out and replaced with the re-dissolved cocaine from the fake pallets and charcoal. These 'special' oranges would be sealed, packaged and boxed and sent via a container ship to Marseilles and onwards to his European partners for distribution.

Everything was in place for the large shipment, apart from the fact that his European financiers needed to be assured that the system worked and wished to test the quality of the product themselves, so Mason was in the process of arranging for them to test a larger sample than the medal. They were to come to his patch in the north-east. He was reticent to send this test sample using his devised supply chain, not wishing to risk alerting the authorities before his enterprise had started in earnest, but rather had developed a different mode of transport for this sample. He had ordered a pallet's worth of cocaine to be shipped to his charcoal imports business in Palma. A small amount was to be re-dissolved and added to plaster and was then to be placed with bandages around the leg of an unsuspecting drug mule, who would then board a plane back to the UK, posing as a tourist returning from a weekend away, having sustained an injury to his leg during an alcohol-fuelled, balcony-jumping incident gone wrong. The Europeans would see the product in its mixed state and a cook would then do his work to allow them to test the purity of the cocaine.

Mason needed someone who had more chance of passing through undetected, someone without a criminal record – and a fall guy, should something go wrong. That guy's name was Jimmy Knox.

Chapter 6

Hard Knox in the Balearics

Ramon ushered the dog handler out of the room and told the remaining Guardia Civil officers to vacate the room. He told Knox to get dressed and turning to James he said,

"Listen James, you need to go now. I thank you for your help here but this is now a police matter and you should go back home. I will get one of my colleagues to join me to interview this guy. Okay? Can you get a taxi and I will sort it out when I see you next?"

"Of course, Ramon. I understand. It's no problem," said James, getting up from his seat.

He left the room and nodded to the Guardia Civil officers outside and made his way to the taxi cab rank outside the Arrivals terminal. He took a taxi back to where he had parked his scooter, just before the Sóller tunnel. He used the taxi ride to try and make sense of what had just happened. He was going over the sequence of events that had just unfolded in his head but this was tinged with a sense of disappointment; disappointment at not being able to interview Knox and to find out exactly what he was going to say and to be able to ask him questions in response. He knew he was no longer a police detective and he was now living in Mallorca where he had no jurisdiction but despite this he still longed to be involved in investigative work of this type. It made it all the harder to swallow as it had been his actions that had led to this investigation in the first place, albeit through a chance encounter.

James consoled himself in the knowledge that in his previous dealings with Ramon, during criminal investigations that he had either uncovered or helped with locally, he had been kept up to date and given privileged information that would not have been normal practice. He realised that Ramon had previously taken risks outside of normal policing protocol to make James as involved as he dared but perhaps now things might be different. Ramon was now in a senior rank and had more to lose. It had been three years since he had had any involvement with James and despite the mutual admiration, both as men and as criminal investigators, James couldn't be sure Ramon would debrief him.

He is under no obligation to tell me anything, he thought to himself, as he was dropped off beside his moped. He returned home to Fornalutx and changed out of his gym wear. He cleaned his injuries with antiseptic ointment and was dabbing his right knee with cotton wool when Charlotte entered the bathroom.

"Oh dear, that doesn't look good," she said, wincing at his badly grazed knee. "How did you do that?" she asked.

"Oh you know, just the usual: catching criminals," smirked James, with a sense of irony.

"What? Go on then, what have you and Ramon been up to? I am really going to have a chat with him and tell him either to start paying you danger money or to stop involving you in his police matters," said Charlotte, shaking her head in disbelief.

"Ramon had nothing to do with this," started James, "Well not at the beginning anyhow. You know I was going to the gym when I left the hotel. Anyway, as I was riding along in Sóller, this numpty steps right out in front of me and I came off the scooter and did this and this," said James, showing her his shoulder injury. "I obviously go and see if he's okay and notice he has his leg in plaster. He tries to get away because he says he has a plane to catch and he gives me dodgy details but he had dropped his wallet. To cut a long story short, I contact Ramon to help me get his wallet to him before his plane leaves and Guardia Civil officers at the airport go to speak to him and he does a runner. Suspicious, obviously. Ramon and I arrive and lo and behold this guy has got a load of drugs down his plaster cast and Ramon's just arrested him and is interviewing him as we speak."

"You are unbelievable. You can't leave this house without getting involved in something. You don't even have to leave the house or the hotel for that matter; you just seem to attract nutters!" said Charlotte, raising her eyebrows.

"I'm not even going to respond to that," said James, continuing to dab his knee. "Anyway, I'm not long in, so I haven't had a chance to make anything for tea. Oh, by the way, I'm going up to Palma in the morning as there's a changeover at the boat."

"I know, don't worry. Magdalena is going there for ten and the guests are due to arrive around one."

"Do you know who is coming?" asked James.

"Someone called Simon Rodgers and his wife. I think he's from the Greater Manchester Police," said Charlotte.

"Okay. Well, I'll get down there for about twelve then to make sure everything is shipshape and then stay for the meet-and-greet."

"That's fine. I'm next door tomorrow but when you get back you can do something with the boys."

After the evening meal on the roof terrace, the family walked down to the plaça at the end of their street. It was the start of the main fiesta in Fornalutx and the whole village was looking very festive and resplendent, with trails of white paper bunting adorning every street light and tree in the village. There was traditional Mallorcan music being performed in the square and as they walked down the main steps, in front of the church, the compact plaça was full of life. It was nearly ten o'clock and there were now very familiar tunes emanating from the musical ensemble.

There were six local musicians playing traditional tunes and beating traditional Mallorcan drums. One played a 'xeremia', a Mallorcan bagpipe made from thick goat skin and cloth. Another played a 'ximbomba', an unusual friction drum with a very unusual sound and with a hint of a phallus about it. The remaining four seemed to have the most to do, as they played a 'flabiol'– a small, five finger-holed, wooded flute – with their left hand, whilst beating a 'tambor', a small drum, with their right hand.

James usually joked to Charlotte that they only had about three songs, as to him, the traditional music sounded very similar. He enjoyed it and was glad to see that this tradition was very much alive and well in this part of Mallorca, although his joke was wearing thin with Charlotte, who was very passionate about this traditional music. The small ensemble or 'colla' would normally play a 'bolero', a 'mateixa', with a more lively meter, a 'copeo' and 'cossiers', which were some of the oldest types of Mallorcan dance songs. Quite often at festivals and fiestas, dancers in traditional, rustic Mallorcan clothing would perform along with the musicians but tonight was just a practice session for later in the week.

During the forty years of the Franco dictatorship, the Spanish government had exercised rigid and unyielding control over the country's non-Castilian cultures. This was no more evident than in folk music and dance. Along with the resurgence of the Catalan language and literature, Mallorca was recovering its once banished traditions.

James and Charlotte managed to get a table outside the busy Bar Deportivo and sat down to appreciate the spectacle. Before long, the attentive and amicable owner Miquel approached.

"¿Hola, que tal? Dime," said Miquel, patting the top of Reuben's head in a show of affection before saying to him, "¿Com va?"

"Molt be," replied Reuben, with an impish grin.

"Una caña para me," replied James.

"Miquel, una copa de vino blanco and dos zumos de naranja para los niños," said Charlotte.

"Muy bien," he said, heading off with their order.

A short time later their drinks arrived with some complementary tapas. Before long, Reuben spotted several of his friends and both he and Adam went off to play further along the plaça. They were playing on a temporary stage which had been set up for the medal ceremony, which would take place the following day, after the conclusion of the running race through the streets of the village. Later, during the village fiesta, James would take part in the village football game; married men against the bachelors. It had been a close fought game the previous year, with the bachelors winning on penalties.

The following week would see the 'running of the bull', where a small, tethered bull would be led through the village and later, it would be humanely slaughtered and the meat distributed to the local people. This was likely to be the last year that this tradition would be permitted, as it had attracted a great deal of opposition from those opposed to what they saw as animal rights violations and it seemed that the local ajuntament, or council, had to comply with new Balearic government rules, culture or not.

There was also the annual village street party, where most of the residents would dine al fresco around numerous dining tables and enjoy a meal, whilst being entertained by musicians, magicians and various street entertainers. James enjoyed the camaraderie of this event, where locals and expat residents sat together as citizens of the village of Fornalutx. The fortnight-long fiesta would culminate with a grand extravaganza at the sports ground, where residents and guests would enjoy more live music on a stage, with food and drink subsidised by the council, ending in a spectacular fireworks display. James took part in as much as he could and felt privileged to live in such a vibrant and welcoming village as Fornalutx.

After enjoying a further round of drinks and chatting to various friends dotted around the tables, James and his family retired for the evening. The following morning he woke to a gentle breeze wafting in through the open windows of his top-floor bedroom. It was a cooler breeze than normal and as he looked out he could see the unusual sight of clouds on this late August morning. He could see chinks of blue sky and knew it wouldn't be long before the hot sun would permeate through the clouds, but for now he lay on in bed enjoying the cooling wind.

Charlotte was already up and next door at the hotel. He could hear his sons in the living room downstairs playing on one of several possible options that came with a screen. He lay on in bed, enjoying the relative peace that he was being afforded when suddenly this was interrupted unceremoniously by the ring tone of his mobile phone and the noise of it vibrating on his bedside table next to him. He picked it up, with half a mind to let it go to voicemail when he saw that the caller was Ramon. James answered the call.

"Good morning Ramon. How goes it?" he asked while checking the time on his mobile and seeing it was just after 8.30am.

"Good morning James. I am sorry to ring you so early but I didn't get much sleep last night and I have been working since six o'clock this morning. Our friend Knox from last night; I think we are onto something pretty big here my friend," started Ramon.

"Why? What did he tell you in the interview?" asked James eagerly, sitting up in bed.

"He is only a small player and he doesn't know that much but it is who he is working for and what we have discovered in the last twelve hours that interests me and the National Crime Agency in the UK. Look, I don't have time to tell you everything now on the phone but I will, I promise. I owe that to you, as you brought him to our attention. Listen James, I have a big favour to ask you. I should not ask you this and you do not have to agree. The situation is that we are allowing Knox to get on a plane today, on a flight back to Newcastle, which leaves at 3.30pm. How would you like a trip back to the UK and an overnight stay in a hotel and then back home tomorrow morning? I would not even ask you if there was any danger involved, which there is not. I have no manpower available from my own unit, as they are needed here at this end because there are at least two premises we are watching and most of my men don't speak English. It is basically to chaperone Knox on the plane from a safe distance and to make sure the NCA surveillance team pick him up at the airport," said Ramon, eventually pausing to wait for James' reaction.

"Wow! I don't know what to say, Ramon. I am quite chuffed you would consider me for such a role. Let me think... Okay, I think I can do it. I need to welcome some police guests coming to stay at the houseboat retreat in Palma Marina around one o'clock and if they are on time I can be at the airport for no later than two o'clock. I just need to let Charlotte know but leave it with me. Where will I meet you?" said James, excited by the prospect of being involved, even in a minor role.

"Okay. You come to the office where we were yesterday and I will brief you in full there. In the meantime, can you text me your details and passport number and I will get your boarding cards for both flights?" asked Ramon.

"No problem. I'll do it straight away. Adiós.¡Hasta luego!" said James.

He jumped out of bed with a mixture of excitement and panic, as the leisurely day that he had planned had just got a little more hectic. He quickly stepped into the shower, got dressed and packed a few items in an overnight bag. He grabbed his passport and furnished Ramon with details by text before going downstairs to instruct his boys to get some breakfast. He then went to the adjoining Hotel Artesa, where Charlotte was still attending to their clients at breakfast service.

"Good morning! Good morning!" he said to his guests, as he entered the courtyard to the rear of the hotel. "Charlotte, can I have a quick word?" said James, beckoning her inside, out of earshot of the guests.

Both went to the reception area of the hotel.

"What's up?" she asked.

"Okay. Here's the thing. Do you know the little matter that Ramon and I were involved in yesterday?" said James, putting out feelers to see how receptive Charlotte was going to be.

"Yes," she said slowly.

"Well, it just so happens that Ramon really needs my help. It is only an overnight thing and he's paying for it and..."

"Paying for what?" interrupted Charlotte, looking bemused.

"He needs me to fly to Newcastle this afternoon and to make sure that a surveillance team picks up a suspect and that's it. I will be put up in a hotel at the airport and the flight gets me back to Palma for one o'clock tomorrow. That's it, job done. I will be back here for two and I will take the boys out when I get back. It just means you would need to cover my shift at the hotel tomorrow and Adam will have to look after Rueben this afternoon. I've already been booked onto the flight and considering everything Ramon has done for us…"

"I don't think I have much say in this, do I? Oh go on then, as long as that's all it is James. I don't think I could cope with anything else, like we had four years ago," said Charlotte in an exasperated tone of voice.

"Don't worry," said James, taking her by the hands in an effort to console her, "I wouldn't put you or the boys through anything like that again. Anyway, I have been craving decent maple-flavoured bacon and I think I will stock up at the nearest Waitrose and try and get some potato bread while I'm at it," he said.

"I wouldn't mind something myself. Surprise me. Alright, let Adam know and I'll see you tomorrow after-noon then," said Charlotte, returning to the breakfast area.

James returned home and appraised Adam of the situation, before setting off to his car with his hand luggage and driving to Palma. He made his way along the main road of Paseo Marítimo in front of Palma's Cathedral of Santa Maria, more commonly known as La Seu and parked on the street. He crossed the road and made his way towards the jetty where his houseboat was moored.

The houseboat had been designed by an interior design team back in the UK, who used a team of boat builders based in Liverpool to build it to their bespoke design. James had an input in the finishing and he was very proud of the end result and so 'Soul is My Ideal Break' or 'Soul' for short was born. It had come about due to James' friend Matt unintentionally involving James in a criminal feud, which didn't end well for those criminals involved but when the dust settled Matt was still in possession of a large amount of untraceable cash that the criminals were unaware he had. Matt had been shot in an effort to protect James and felt that the money would be wasted if simply returned to Spanish police, as it was the proceeds of crime. In the end, after a lot of soul- searching, James decided his 'share' of the money would still go back to the police, in a way, but he would act as custodian and put it to a more fitting use, hence the purchase of the houseboat.

He had set up a registered charity and 'Soul' was to be an 'R&R' destination for serving police officers who required some respite from the rigours of their professional life, whether they were suffering from physical issues or from stress-related problems. It was busy throughout most of the year and the only thing the various police associations had to do was make a small payment, which covered the mooring fee and the cleaning after each stay. It was such a popular destination that James had now limited the maximum stay to five nights to allow as many police officers as possible to take advantage of the prime location.

He arrived at the end of the jetty to see Magdalena, the cleaner, moping the top deck.

"Buenas tardes, Magdalena," said James, as he approached.

"Oh, buenas tardes, James," she replied, looking at her watch and realising it was after twelve.

"¿Todo bien? Everything is good?" he asked.

"Sí, sí, sí. Todo bien. I am now finished," she said, wiping her brow and smiling and ringing out the mop.

"¡Perfecto! Todo se ve bien," said James, looking around at the gleaming deck and nodding.

"He terminado. I am finished. ¡Hasta luego, James!" said Magdalena.

"Gracias Magdalena. Hasta la próxima. Adiós."

James looked around the spacious top deck with a sense of pride. The charcoal-coloured boat was moored just off Palma's main marina and his guests had the spectacular vista of all the gleaming yachts, boats and superyachts, and the open sea beyond, in one direction. In the other, they had the beautiful gothic cathedral and the numerous other period city buildings and avenues of this compact gem of a city. The deck was already dry after being cleaned and James walked along the spacious deck and took a seat on one of the two outdoor sofas under the shade of a large parasol. He had stayed on the two-bedroomed boat with his family when it first arrived but they had not had many further opportunities since then, due to it being so popular and due to James not wishing to disappoint those he felt were more in need of a break that himself. Taking in the views of the location, he vowed that he would reserve at least a weekend for his family, later in the year.

James wandered below deck to the spacious accommodation. He stepped into the bright, open-plan living area with kitchen and dining area beyond. He was keen on interior design and he had picked geometric, encaustic grey and white tiles that adorned the floor and the splashback above the Belfast sink. The grey-washed timber boards on the walls helped reflect the light and gave the interior a Swedish-Gustavian style, but the more modern pieces of furniture and designer lighting gave it a contemporary feel. It had a separate double bedroom, a small second room with bunk beds, and a shower room. The living area had a feature wood-burning stove which made it a very cosy hideaway in the cooler months.

He checked that the welcome pack had been topped up. There were oranges and paté from Sóller, chocolate, breadsticks, eggs, sobrasada, Mallorcan wine and mineral water, beer and soft drinks. He checked that Magdalena had left sufficient coffee pods for the coffee machine and that everything was in order. As usual, it was and James realised that he was fortunate in having someone as rigorous and dependable as Magdalena.

He stepped up to the deck again to await the arrival of his guests, who were flying in from Manchester Airport. James just hoped their flight had not been delayed, so he checked online and found it had landed on time. He needed to leave soon to give himself plenty of time to park at the airport and to be briefed by Ramon.

He didn't have long to wait, as he could see a couple walking towards the boat dragging two suitcases behind them. James welcomed his guests, who were visibly more than happy with their accommodation and its location and he wished them a relaxing break, before heading back to his car and setting off for Palma Airport.

After parking his car in the multi-storey carpark, James made his way to the police office where he was to meet Ramon. He knocked on the door, which was opened by a Guardia Civil officer and James could see Ramon already seated inside but in conversation on his mobile phone and on seeing James, motioned with his hand to the officer to let him in. James took a seat at the table. Ramon remained in conversation for a few more minutes before greeting him.

"James, thank you for this, my friend. I appreciate it and at such late notice but you wouldn't believe how busy it has been here after your friend Knox's revelations. First things first: here are your boarding tickets for both flights. Also, I have made you a reservation at the Hilton Hotel at Newcastle Airport for tonight. Any other expenses that you incur, I would ask you to keep the receipts and I will pay you from my operational police budget when you get back.

"Okay. This guy Knox, according to the NCA, has no previous criminal record. He says he was sent here to collect a sample of cocaine by his boss, who is well-known to the authorities. Knox told me that he owed this guy money and this was the only way he could get away with not being put in hospital. The cocaine was not inside the plaster cast: it *was* the plaster cast. He was picked up by a guy at the airport and then driven to a warehouse at the docks in Palma. We have got a team watching it as we speak. He says that when he was there, he saw a pallet being broken up and then he was taken by car into the mountains, as he called it. He said he went through a long tunnel and described the journey he took. He went to a small house, where another guy, who was also English, dissolved the bits of pallet. Knox said he mixed it with plaster and then with bandages. He then wrapped the whole thing around Knox's leg until it was set. He slept at the house and described it as overlooking a village with orange trees around it and that there was a metal sheep or cattle grid at the long entrance to the house. We think we have got the right property and have another team on it, between Fornalutx and Biniaraix.

"Knox was on his way to the airport, when he stepped out in front of you in Sóller. He was then driven to the airport by the warehouse guy, and he was to meet his boss yesterday after being picked up at Newcastle

Airport. Obviously he didn't make that flight but after the interview we allowed him to leave. He says he will cooperate with us fully but he is very scared. Scared of us, but also frightened about what will happen if these major drug guys find out where our information came from. He doesn't know it but we have placed a tracking device in the lining of his wallet. We got him to ring his boss in the UK and explain that he had been involved in an accident and that he had missed his flight and that he would get the same flight today. Luckily there were a few seats left. I don't think his boss suspects anything, as his driver confirmed that he had been hit by a scooter yesterday.

"Knox was then picked up by the same driver from the airport yesterday. We tailed the car to the olivar where he stayed last night again, and I have just heard that they have left and are heading in the direction of the airport. I have been liaising with the NCA, who now believe Knox's boss is looking to bring in a very large shipment of cocaine bound for the European market, and this is a sample of the broken pallet product in preparation for a large order. We know the olivar was bought very recently in a company name of a business based in the British Virgin Islands and it is supposedly an orange exporter.

"The warehouse in Palma is being rented by a company calling itself Charcoal Imports (Majorca) Limited, again with its headquarters in the British Virgin Islands, both obviously fronts for their criminal enterprise. Your job, James, is simply to be our eyes and ears on the plane so as to not arouse suspicion, in case Knox is travelling with an accomplice we don't know about. Your seat is quite far from his. He knows he will be followed and he accepts this as part of the offer I made to him but he knows the consequences if he fucks up. We have taken an evidential sample from the cast – he has told his boss it was broken when he was hit by the moped.

"Once he gets off the plane, he will go through passport control. The NCA team will pick him up from there and follow him to the handover. We know the shipment won't come in unless this sample gets through, which is why he is being allowed to take it back to the UK. Neither we nor the NCA yet know who all the players are in this as it is such fresh information, but we are learning more by the minute.

"If there are any problems you can ring me on my mobile and I will contact our NCA friends. They don't know you are on the flight. It is better for you that they don't. I didn't want you having to give evidence in any future trial. Charlotte would never speak to me again, and it is not exactly doing things 'by the book', as you used to call it. Is there anything you want to ask me James?" said Ramon, looking at his watch.

"No, I don't think so Ramon. Are you happy he is going to play ball?" asked James.

"As you know, you can never be one hundred per cent happy with these people, which is why I need you to make sure Knox gets to passport control. After that, he's not your problem."

"That's fine," said James, standing up.

"¡Venga! Good luck. Have a nice flight and I will see you tomorrow on your safe return to Mallorca. Adios James," said Ramon, giving James a smile and a firm handshake.

James left the office and made his way to the departures area, through airport security and then onward to

Departure Gate A. His actual flight gate was due to be displayed in about thirty minutes, so he relaxed with a coffee and looked out for Knox. Twenty minutes later, Knox arrived and joined the queue at a nearby Burger King and James watched him sit down at a table with his food. His demeanour seemed calm for someone in his position, although he appeared to be looking around him more than would be usual but James put this down to Knox being made aware that he would be followed.

An announcement came over the public address system that his flight to Newcastle was leaving from Gate 10. James watched Knox make his way towards the gate. He deliberated whether it was better for Knox to know he was following him or not and he concluded that it would give him the upper hand if Knox didn't see him but not the end of the world if he did. James hung back whilst keeping Knox in sight. He had allowed for the possibility of Knox being watched by a member of the criminal gang, to make sure Knox was following orders, especially in light of the fact that he had missed the flight the previous day. James felt that if he was the drug kingpin behind this operation, he would definitely be very suspicious of a guy like Knox not making his flight as instructed, no matter what the circumstances.

The announcement to board the EasyJet flight was made and James allowed Knox to get into the queue to board. Once Knox had gone through toward the plane he joined the back of the queue and showed his passport and boarding card. He would be sitting in 22c, an aisle seat towards the back of the plane. As passengers were boarding from the front of the plane only, James thought it likely that Knox would see him and recognise him, unless positioned even further back along the plane than James. It was at that point that James wished Ramon had told him exactly where Knox's seat was but it wasn't crucial. James slipped on his prescription sunglasses that were resting on his head and entered the plane, showing his boarding card to the flight attendant. He walked down the aisle and saw Knox, who had settled into his seat and was looking down at the in-flight magazine and James passed by him unnoticed. He put his case in the overhead locker and took his seat.

The flight was uneventful, apart from when James switched off for a minute to enjoy an in-flight drink. Before he knew it, Knox was in the middle of the aisle limping his way along in his direction, without the use of his crutch. James bent down as if he was picking something up, as Knox passed him on the way to the rear toilet. James quickly changed his sunglasses for his ordinary glasses and put them on and retook his seat. A short time later, Knox walked back past him and re-took his seat, without casting a glance towards James.

The flight landed on time and he arrived to a grey and wet afternoon in Newcastle Airport. James was content that all he had to do was keep eyes on his target until through passport control and then the time was his own. He was allowing his mind to ponder whether to eat in the hotel itself or to take a taxi into Newcastle city centre and enjoy some fine dining and a nice bottle of wine. He could see Knox exit the aircraft so now he was out of sight. It seemed to take an awfully long time for the people in the rows behind Knox to do the same but eventually James disembarked from the aircraft directly into the airport and he hurriedly passed as many passengers as he could in an effort to regain his sight of Knox. He was beginning to get nervous, because he couldn't see him amongst the crowd of passengers heading towards passport control, until he caught a glimpse of him, as Knox glanced sideways. James realised that he had taken off his beige-coloured baseball cap, which he was now carrying and he was now close enough to confirm it was Knox. He saw him limp along on his crutch and he could now see the plaster cast was missing a small piece from the back.

That must be where Ramon took it from, thought James, relieved that his job would soon be over. He moved into a position to see clearly from about twenty people back from him, as Knox was asked to step forward to a passport control officer. He could see the UK border control officer smile, as he surmised that he and Knox were in conversation about his leg being in plaster. Knox was then handed his passport and he walked on through, heading towards Baggage Reclaim and the exit and out of his view. James' job was over, as he knew the surveillance team would now be following Knox within the airport and they had the tracking device as a back-up, so he could now enjoy his mini break.

Chapter 7

The Best-Laid Plans
of Mice and Men

James moved closer to the three border control booths and was directed to the middle one and handed over his passport. The female officer scanned his passport and made him look straight ahead to allow the camera to get a clear view of his face.

"Did you have a nice holiday?" she asked in a routine manner.

"I live over in Mallorca. I'm having a short break here," he replied.

"Lucky you. I mean, living over there like," she said smiling, before handing him back his passport.

James walked on, wheeling his hand luggage case behind him, stopping briefly to put his passport in his case. He looked ahead for signs for a toilet as his bladder was now reminding him of the red wine he had drunk on the plane. He saw a sign for the toilets and used the facilities. He thought about ringing Ramon but decided he would wait until he could find more privacy outside the airport. He stopped and ordered a large cappuccino to go from Starbucks and walked towards the exit. He stopped to take a swig from his plastic cup, when he noticed two men on either side of the concourse. They were on their own but both were staring intently in the same direction. James followed their gaze to another entrance to toilets. From his position of about fifty metres away, he could clearly see an earpiece in the left ear of one of the men. Their demeanour, their age, height and build, as well as their casual but awkward dress sense, said only one thing to him: undercover police.

James had had first-hand experience of this, having worked as a plain clothes officer in both the drug squad and in CID. He had also worked undercover in test purchase operations, where he had to blend in with drug dealers and users. He had always made an effort to blend in but felt that some police officers would look like police officers, no matter what they wore. The two men he was looking at right at that moment might as well have been in full uniform with a flashing blue light on their heads, as far as he was concerned. He felt that the only explanation for them watching the toilets was that Knox must be inside, so he felt obliged to wait and see the outcome and to confirm his suspicions about his 'boys in blue'.

A few minutes passed and James could see both officers communicate with each other via their covert radios, which gave even more credence to his suspicions. They appeared to be nervous and one, in particular, was becoming visibly agitated. Just then, Knox exited from the toilet, wearing his beige baseball cap and carrying his small burgundy case. He walked out of the exit quickly and out of sight of James, followed sharply by both of the undercover officers. James could still see them communicating with each other and he walked outside to see them following Knox; one on either side of the footpath, heading towards the long stay car park.

It was only then that James realised that Knox's leg was no longer in plaster.

He must have broken it up and put it in his case, thought James. *But why would he do that and risk someone coming into the toilets and reporting him to the police? It didn't make sense,* he thought, as he realised that he hadn't actually seen Knox's face when he had exited the toilets at quite a fast pace. James was beginning to feel uneasy. Knox or someone in Knox's clothing and both officers had turned a corner and were no longer in view. He was trying to decide whether to ring Ramon or go and check the toilets, when from behind him he heard the automatic doors open and a man started walking in the direction of several cars in the drop-off zone. James could only see the man from behind but his height, size and hair colour fitted Knox. He was wearing different clothing and carrying a rucksack over his right shoulder but James was pretty sure that this man was Knox.

What the hell is he playing at? he thought, as he watched the man approach a black Porsche Cayenne with tinted windows, and for a split second before the man got into the front passenger seat, James saw the man's face, side on.

"Shit! It is him!" he mumbled to himself.

James began to panic. The car had its engine running and was indicating to pull out. He quickly ran towards a taxi rank further up the road, closer to the exit.

He jumped into the taxi at the front of the line, just as the black Porsche passed.

"Where to mate?" asked the taxi driver.

"Follow that black Porsche!" demanded James. "I'll explain on the way."

The taxi driver looked at James in his internal mirror and pulled out before saying,

"I can only do the legal speed limit, mind."

James could see the Porsche about a hundred metres away and it was now stationary at a set of traffics light on red. The taxi driver pulled in behind it. James pulled his wallet out of his pocket and checked inside. He had £40 sterling and €100 in cash. He thought briefly, just as the traffic lights turned to green, before saying,

"Look, here's what it is mate. I'm a private detective and my client thinks his missus has been having an affair with a younger man and he's just come off a plane from Mallorca and I need to find out who he is. Now I'll give you all the cash I have on me if you keep up with that car. I've got £40 and €100 in cash," said James, handing the cash to the driver.

"Alright then mate. I'll do my best for you."

"Thank you. My client and I really appreciate it," said James.

He quickly pulled out his mobile phone and rang Ramon.

"James. Where are you? The team think they have lost Knox…"

"Listen, Ramon!" interrupted James, "I am in a minicab heading…where are we heading driver?" asked James.

"It looks as if we're heading towards Sunderland city centre," said the taxi driver.

"I am heading in the direction of Sunderland and Knox is in a black Porsche Cayenne, registration number alpha mike six eight four five, which would appear to be a personalised number plate. Is the tracker not working?" asked James.

"I can't believe these stupid English idiots cannot do a simple job! No, I am told the tracking device has not worked or he has discovered it and thrown it away. What I am being told is that Knox came through passport control…"

"They are turning into the Lambton Worm," said the taxi driver.

"Wait a minute Ramon," said James.

"Do you want me to go into the car park as well or stay here?" asked the taxi driver, who had pulled over by a footpath.

"Just wait here for a second," said James, as he watched Knox and two men get out of their car and go into the Wetherspoon's public house.

"Ramon, he's gone into a pub called the Lambton Worm on…hang on."

"On Low Road, Sunderland, near the Empire Theatre," said the taxi driver.

"On Low Road, Sunderland, near the Empire Theatre," repeated James.

"Okay. Okay, I got it. I will ring these idiots now and tell them to go there. Can you wait there, James? Is it safe for you?" asked Ramon.

"Yes. No problem. I'll wait here," said James.

"I will ring you back once they tell me how long it will take to get there. Okay James? Adios."

"Adios."

"Are you okay to wait for a few minutes, mate?" asked James.

"That's not a problem," said the taxi driver. "Your money is still good for a little while yet."

James' mobile rang.

"Well? How long?" asked James.

"They say they are about fifteen minutes away. They are still at the airport. They had just taken the decision to stop the guy who came out of the toilets without the plaster cast on his leg. Apparently, Knox went into the toilets and bribed a guy to change clothes with him for €500. The guy said Knox broke off his plaster cast and they swapped bags. Knox told him to walk out of the toilets and head for the long stay car park. Anyway, they now know they haven't got the right man, so I had to tell them about your involvement. They will be arriving in two black BMW 5 series cars. Ring me when they arrive please James," asked Ramon.

"Okay, will do."

James came off the phone and waited for the surveillance team to arrive. He didn't like waiting and he didn't like not knowing what was happening inside the pub. He couldn't understand Knox's logic. He knew Knox would realise he would be extradited for the drug offences and wondered if he just hadn't got cold feet. He was obviously more scared of those who had sent him in the first place. If he told those who had sent him what had happened the drug shipment would never arrive in Mallorca and they might lose all hope of catching the big fish in this crime network.

Perhaps he hasn't told them yet. Perhaps, he's not planning to, thought James.

He couldn't just sit there waiting any longer. James said to the taxi driver,

"Thanks for your help. I'll take it from here."

James heard the door lock release and the taxi driver said,

"Good luck mate."

James got out and carried his case towards the front door of the pub as the taxicab drove off. He stood outside momentarily wondering whether he should wait outside or go inside and see what was happening. James had already chosen the second option in his head before he had got out of the taxi, and with a deep intake of breath he opened the door to the pub and walked inside.

He took a few seconds to get his bearings inside. It was relatively dark and he could see about twenty people sitting at tables, some eating and some drinking. The majority of the clientele were men. James couldn't see Knox. He noticed two very stocky men at a table drinking and he was sure that these were the men he had seen exiting the Porsche Cayenne with Knox. He walked further into the pub but there was still no sign of Knox. He saw a sign for the toilets and walked towards them. As he opened the door he saw Knox washing his hands at the wash hand basins. Knox looked in the mirror and immediately recognised James. James walked inside as Knox turned around to him.

"Ah for fuck's sake mate, I can't take any more of this. I never wanted to get involved in any of this," said Knox, distraughtly.

James put his finger up to his mouth.

"There's nobody else in here," said Knox.

"Listen Jimmy, don't be stupid. This won't go away. You made a deal and this is your best chance of having a life. You can't just walk away and hope it all turns out fine. Have you told those guys out there anything?" said James, quietly.

"No, I've told them fuck all. We came in here to get a bite to eat before the boss wants us to meet him, like. I have no fuckin' intention of telling them anything about it. I want to continue breathing you know," said Knox, trying but failing to crack a smile.

"Listen, your only chance is to do what you said you would do for Ramon in Mallorca. You are in the shit big time if you don't and you are going to end up inside for something you have done under duress. You will get protection, a new identity, if needs be. Think about it for a second. Do the right thing. The cops are already outside again so there's nowhere to run. Just keep quiet and everything will be alright. Okay?" asked James.

"Aye, fuck it. I don't have much choice, do I?" said Knox.

Just then, the door behind James opened and he turned round to see one of the two burly men, who had been in the Porsche, walk in. He gave James a stern look.

"Everything alright here, Jimmy?"

"Aye man, he was just askin' if I could get him some snow, like," said Knox.

"Oh aye and who the fuck are you?" said the burly man, now standing very close to James with his fists clenched.

"I'm just looking to score some coke for my mate's stag do. I'm not from round here, as you can probably tell, so can you help me out or what?" asked James, realising that he had no cash left.

"Fuck off before I lose my temper. Jimmy outside now!" barked the burly man, eyeballing James, while Jimmy walked out of the toilets, followed by his minder, leaving James alone.

James breathed a sigh of relief. He didn't fancy his chances with a guy who he reckoned was about eighteen stones and clearly had a steroid dependency, judging by his bulked-up appearance. James could handle himself where necessary but he was in a confined gents toilets, and there was an equally bulky associate of the steroid guy a few feet away, and James was a realist.

James walked out of the gents and saw the three men back at their table. The steroid guy stared at him, until James looked away. He contemplated walking straight out of the pub, but although this was very appealing to him he thought it might look even more suspicious than going to the bar, so he opted to go to the bar and ordered a pint of lager.

"That's £2.25 please mate," said the barman, reaching James his pint.

James inserted his debit card into the card machine, got his receipt and sat down at a table outside. He could see a black BMW 5 series car now in the carpark and another one further down the street. He took a sip of his beer, sat down and quickly pulled out his mobile phone and rang Ramon.

"Ramon, it's me. I can see the two BMWs and I'm outside the pub. Listen, I have just been inside and I spoke to Knox..." started James.

"You did what?" shouted Ramon.

"It's okay. Listen, I spoke to him in the toilets. He had a wobble but he's back on side. I don't think he's said anything to the two guys he's with. He's scared but I think I talked him round."

"James, James my friend. What were you thinking? You could have compromised the operation, or worse, you could have got badly injured," said Ramon with passion.

"I know. It was a judgement call and I had to make it. Knox said they just called in to get something to eat and they are then going to meet the boss. I was scared he might tell these guys what had happened but I don't think he will now. I'm sorry but I thought it was the right thing to do," said James.

There was a short pause before Ramon said,

"Let's hope it was the right thing to do. James, I want you to leave now and go to your hotel. I can't afford for you to get involved in this anymore than you have been. What was I thinking? Please James, promise me you will leave now and go to your hotel. These guys could be armed for all we know. They are not small-time dealers, these guys are major league criminals."

"Okay. I promise, just after I finish my pint. It might look suspicious if they see that I've left a full pint when they come outside," replied James.

"¡Jésus, José y Maria! Finish it in, how do you say, 'down in one'!" started Ramon, before adding, "Por favor, James."

James raised his glass and drank his pint of lager in several large gulps, causing him to belch upon finishing.

"Okay. I'm leaving now. I'll ring you later. Bye."

James lifted his small case and walked along the street, giving a casual nod to the occupants of one of the black BMW cars, who did not reciprocate the gesture. He walked until he came to a cashpoint and withdrew some sterling from his bank account before hailing a passing taxi and making his way back towards Newcastle Airport and to the Hilton Hotel nearby, where he checked in.

Chapter 8

A Waiting Game

A few days after James' impromptu flying visit back to 'Blighty', he was at the reception desk in Hotel Artesa, when an English couple in their late thirties walked in and approached him.

"Good morning. Do you speak English?" they asked.

"Yes, after a fashion," said James, smiling.

"Oh good," said the man. "We're having difficulty in finding the finca we have booked for a fortnight's holiday. Do you recognise this property?"

James looked down on the counter as the man scrolled to a page with photos on a website. The man then scrolled through various photos on his Android phone.

"Stop. Go back one," said James, as he thought he recognised the property from an exterior shot. "I know that house. It is on the other side of the torrent. You cross over the bridge and head up the road for about five hundred metres and there is a set of black gates. They belong to that property. I didn't realise that was available to rent. I heard the owner, who I think is American, was selling it. It has been on the market for a couple of years now but perhaps he has decided to do holiday rentals in the meantime. Who did you book it with?" asked James.

"We booked it through HomeAway, the holiday rental company. We are here with Laura's parents and our two kids but they are in the square having a drink, while we attempt to find this place. We were sent details of where it is supposed to be but it shows it here," said the man, showing James a print out from Google Maps.

"No, it is nowhere near there. Who is your contact and where are you to meet?" asked James.

"It just said 'property manager' and we have been conducting all communication by e-mail. We were due to meet at the property about half an hour ago, so we had better make our way there. Thanks very much for your help. So from here?"

"Drive down the lower street past the plaça, called Carrer de sa Font and continue over a bridge. The road starts to climb and after about five hundred metres you will see a large set of black gates with an intercom buzzer on it. That's your villa," said James.

"Thanks again. What a lovely hotel you have here," said the woman, before both waved and walked back into the street.

James continued with his duties. He had come back from Newcastle and had spoken to Ramon on a couple of occasions since his return. He had gleaned from Ramon that it appeared that Knox had kept his word and had allowed his tailing surveillance team to follow him to the hand- over of his merchandise. Knox was still being monitored but it looked as if his part was now over. He would possibly be required to give evidence at a later trial, although he didn't know it yet.

The NCA had round-the-clock surveillance teams monitoring the movements of all major players, after they were seen at a meeting testing the sample, and various Dutch and Belgian representatives of major crime and drug syndicates with considerable financial clout were seen there. Ramon had teams in place in Mallorca and all agencies concerned believed there was a very large shipment on its way. It was only a matter of time and a waiting game. Ramon had promised to keep James informed of any new developments and James felt honoured that his old friend was prepared to go out on a limb to keep him in the loop.

The hotel was still full to capacity and the early September temperatures were proving to be even hotter than those of July and August. Even with the reception area in shade and with the air conditioning on, James felt a little fatigued and lethargic. He took a bottle of sparkling water from the minibar and poured it into a large glass. He added several ice cubes which clinked against the glass and then cracked instantaneously as they hit the water. He took several long mouthfuls, pausing only to swirl the ice cubes in the glass to decrease the temperature of the water and him further. As he raised the glass to his mouth for another round of refreshment, the glass doors to the hotel opened and in walked the English couple who had earlier stopped for directions.

"Well, any luck?" asked James, setting his glass down.

"We're not sure. We went to where you said and buzzed on the intercom but there was no reply. We have been ringing a Spanish mobile number that we were given but it just keeps going to voicemail. Brian here climbed over the gates and had a look around," said the woman.

"Yeah. I got fed up waiting so I climbed over the gate. It is definitely the right place but it is locked up and as Laura says, we can't get hold of this manager on the phone number provided. It's now nearly five o'clock and we were supposed to have access three hours ago. The kids are getting fed up and to be honest, so am I," said Brian, wiping sweat from his brow.

"Look, I tell you what," said James, "let me ring a friend of mine who works for a local estate agency that has that property on their books and see if they have another contact number for the owner or his manager."

James rang his friend Steve at a local estate agent's office.

"Hi Steve, James here. How goes it?"

"Good James and you? Busy no doubt?" asked Steve.

"Very busy here Steve. Listen, I have a couple in with me at the moment who are having trouble gaining access to a villa they have rented for two weeks through HomeAway. They have a manager's number but it keeps going to voicemail and the property is locked up. The reason I am ringing you is just on the off chance you might have another phone number for the owner or his manager. It is the villa with the infinity pool in Fornalutx with the black gates up the mountain overlooking the village. You have it on your books. Do you know the one I mean?" asked James.

"Yeah, I know the one you mean. I just sold it last week. That house has never been rented and the new owners are not renting it out. They want to make some alterations to it. It sounds as if the people you have with you have been scammed. I have heard that a few people have been caught out in the valley this year. Sorry mate," said Steve sincerely.

"Oh no. Well, thanks for your help and regards to Dolly."

James put the phone down and turned to his now anxious couple who had been hanging on his every word during his phone conversation.

"It doesn't look good. My friend Steve has just told me that the property there on HomeAway has just been sold. It had never been rented out by the previous owner and the new owners are getting ready to make alterations to the property, so he thinks it is a scam," said James apologetically.

Laura winced, as if in pain.

"Well what are we going to do now?" she pleaded.

"It's not this man's problem Laura. We'll have to sort it out," said Brian, shaking his head.

"I would like to help in any way that I can. What you need to do is contact HomeAway immediately and explain what has happened. We use them and other websites like Airbnb, Holiday Lettings and Owners Direct, which is a sister company of HomeAway. The difference with those companies is that to stop this sort of thing from happening, your payment does not go to the purported property owner until about five working days after the guests' arrival date. With HomeAway the owner gets fifty per cent long before the guests arrive and the balance forty-five days before the guests arrive. How much did you pay for your two-week stay?" James asked.

"In total, it was about £5000," said Brian.

"Don't worry, you will get your money back but the scammers will have had the money paid out to them. They tend to go for high-value properties so they can maximise their money, and even if they do it twice before being discovered it is still a tidy sum – replicate that countless times over different fraudulent listings and you have got a nice little enterprise going. The scammers can be based anywhere in the world but Nigeria is a favourite for this kind of thing."

"You seem to know a lot about it," said Laura.

"I used to be a police detective and obviously I'm in the holiday business now, so I like to keep my ear to the ground. You will need to let the local police know about it as well but first I suggest you ring HomeAway so they can help you find alternative accommodation and to compensate you, but also to close down the bogus listing. Let me check the website. Here it is. Ring this number," said James, showing Brian.

Brian dialled the number and managed to get through to someone. James started to scroll through the fake listing on the website and dialled the Spanish mobile number listed for the manager but again it went straight to a Movistar generic message. He scrolled through the photographs and realised that the exterior and interior photographs had simply been taken from the estate agency website by the scammers. He scrolled on to find some additional photos showing more places in the area, which made James think that these must have been taken from someone else's listing but then he stopped and zoomed in on one particular photograph.

"That's my leg!" he shouted.

James had zoomed in on one particular photo of the picturesque plaça in Fornalutx, showing people sitting around the various cafés and bars with a partial figure of a man in the foreground showing mostly his leg and a tennis racquet.

"This is a recent photo. You know, I remember this being taken. I think I know who took it. That is me there," said James, showing it to Brian who had just finished his phone call.

"Are you sure?" asked Brian, not understanding how James could tell just from a shot of a man's leg.

"The reason I know it's me, is the training shoes, the shape of the leg, the tennis racquet. That was the day a friend of mine and I played Rafa Nadal at tennis. It is not a day I will forget. We came back to celebrate with a few beers and I remember this guy who lives in the village was taking quite a few photos with his mobile phone. We even stood up in a triumphant pose, telling him we had just played against Rafa Nadal. I think his name is Enrique or something. I don't know him but I know a guy who does and I think he is originally from Galicia but he has been renting a flat in the village for a few months."

James was becoming suspicious. He thought he would give Enrique the benefit of the doubt and scrolled through all the photos of Fornalutx rental properties and then typed in 'photos of Fornalutx plaça' in Google and checked through numerous photos until he came to the photo in question. He visited the page where it was from which took him directly to the HomeAway site, which meant that it hadn't been uploaded from another website. James' suspicions grew. He decided to ring one of his footballing friends who worked in the village.

"Hey Ricardo, que tal?" he asked.

"Hey hombre, I am good. Is there football this week?" asked Ricardo.

"It is hot but I think we can still play. Listen Ricardo, what do you call your friend who lives in the village who always wears sunglasses, the guy from Galicia?"

"You mean Enrique?" asked Ricardo.

"Yes, that's him. I thought his name was Enrique. Do you have a mobile number for him?" asked James.

"Yeah, I will text it to you. Why do you want his number? He is a little 'loco'," said Ricardo laughing.

"He took a photo of me in the plaça after I played Rafa Nadal and I would like a copy," said James, thinking on his feet.

"You played Rafa at tennis?" said Ricardo, sounding surprised.

"Yeah! Did I not tell…" started James, before realising Ricardo was being ironic, as it had been James' favourite topic of conversation at football for a couple of weeks.

"Adiós amigo," said Ricardo, laughing.

A few seconds later, a text from Ricardo arrived and James looked at the telephone number he had sent for Enrique. It was the same number that was listed for the manager of the villa.

"Any luck from HomeAway?" asked James.

"Yes. I explained the situation and they said not to worry. They have suspended the listing and have asked us to report it to the local police. They have asked us to find a hotel for tonight and they will try and find us another villa for the remainder of our holiday. It's not great but it's better than losing five grand," said Brian.

"I'm going to ring a police friend of mine, as I think I know who might be involved in this. He may not want to deal with it but he can point you in the right direction," said James, lifting the phone.

"Hola, James. There have not been any developments," started Ramon.

"No, no. That's not why I'm calling. Which department would I need to contact if I had a lead on scammers who had defrauded a couple or a company out of about €6000?" asked James.

"Is it a one-off crime or is it more organised?" asked Ramon.

"I don't know, Ramon. I have an English couple here who have been ripped off with a bogus holiday rental and I think I may know someone who's involved," said James.

"Look, since it is you, I will send one of my guys over and he can pass it on if he doesn't think it is something of interest for us but I do know that Jordi, who works for me, was working on something like this recently. He's on duty, so I will send him to your hotel in about an hour. Okay?" asked Ramon.

"You're a star or eres una estrella, I should say!"

James turned to the couple.

"Do you want to come back here in an hour? I have a detective on his way and he can take your complaint and he will need a statement from you. I will also give him the information I have. In the meantime, why don't you have a drink in the square and I will ring a couple of the local hotels and see if they have got rooms for the six of you for tonight," said James, lifting the phone to ring.

"Thank you very much for your help. I don't even know your name."

"James. James Gordon. I am full here otherwise I would have gladly put you up. Leave it with me and check back in an hour."

"Will do. Thanks again. See you later," they said, waving on their way out.

An hour later, Ramon's officer Jordi arrived and James provided him with the information he had. The English couple returned to the hotel and regaled the officer with their unfortunate tale. After getting as much information as they could provide, Jordi left saying he would investigate the crime himself, as he was working on several similar cases across the island. James had managed to get the family three rooms for the night at Ca'n Reus Hotel in the village and wished them luck in finding accommodation for the rest of their holiday. Brian and Laura then presented him with a bottle of cava as a thank you for all his help. James finished his shift at the hotel slightly later than usual and walked the few steps home next door, content that he had been able to help.

Chapter 9

Set a 'Thief Catcher'
to Catch a Thief

Over the next couple of weeks, James was busy dealing with the comings and goings of guests at Hotel Artesa. September was proving to be just as busy as July and August had been. The village itself and the whole Sóller Valley was close to filling its capacity of tourist beds, the only difference from a month earlier was that the majority were devoid of children. The new school term had started all over Europe and families were back in their respective homes dreaming of their return to the magical Sóller Valley. His own boys, Adam and Reuben, had started back at their respective schools and a sense of routine had returned to James' life. He nonetheless was feeling unsettled. He had not heard from Ramon but was reticent to pester him with phone calls enquiring as to any news regarding the drug operation. Ramon had promised him he would be kept in the loop and James knew Ramon was a man of his word.

It was the more recent turn of events regarding the resident of the village, Enrique that was making James uncomfortable. He had hoped to have heard the news by now that he had been arrested and charged with fraud but to date he had heard nothing from Ramon's colleague Jordi. What made things worse was the fact that since he was aware of Enrique's likely involvement in the scam, he was seeing him on an almost daily basis, whereas before he might have been lucky to see him once a fortnight since his arrival from Galicia several months previously. He was now begrudgingly feeling it necessary to acknowledge him with a returning wave or a head nod.

James had been making some low-key enquiries of his own about Enrique through friends and acquaintances. He was mindful that he didn't want to step on Jordi's toes in his investigation, or give Enrique a 'head's up' making him leave the island. He was proving to be a bit of an enigma. On the one hand, he had heard that Enrique was a charming and pleasant guy who did some voluntary work for a charity in Sóller, and on the other hand, that he liked to drink and was very volatile. Either way, James' gut told him that all was not right with him and the evidence trail was leading directly to Enrique's door.

James finished for the day at the hotel and decided to have a relaxing beer in the plaça before preparing the evening meal. He liked to cook and felt they were well-placed on the Mediterranean island to enjoy the natural bounty of the fresh produce available. His son Reuben had now acquired a very Mallorcan palate. He enjoyed sobrasada and honey, fresh tomato with garlic on toast and he would eat fresh figs and have 'jamón ibérico' every day, if he could. James finished his beer and decided to get ingredients for a mixed paella that he would cook on the roof terrace, and so wandered into the small supermarket on the corner of the plaça. As he did, he noticed Enrique standing at the butcher's counter at the rear of the shop and not wanting to engage him in conversation James turned around and left the shop without purchasing anything and walked up the steps that skirted the plaça and home.

He was annoyed that he felt it necessary to avoid this 'criminal' so close to his home and it was stopping him from going about his daily life. James went to his study on the first floor and pressed the speed dial button for Ramon.

"James, my friend. I was just talking about you earlier. Nothing bad, don't worry. Just to give you an update about the shipment. We know it left Cartagena about three weeks ago and is due to dock in Palma in another three weeks after making several stops along the way. I will let you know of any results, I promise," said Ramon.

"I know you will Ramon but that's not why I called. I wanted to know if Jordi had made any progress regarding the fraud case he is working on. To be honest, I didn't want to bother him directly but it's been two weeks and I keep seeing the guy Enrique all over the village and it's making me uncomfortable. Do you know where he is at with it?" asked James.

"¡Me encanta este chico!" said Ramon into the phone but he was obviously speaking to others present at his end as well, who James could hear laughing.

"James, I was saying 'I just love this guy' because we were wondering how long it would be before you rang about this case. I love your enthusiasm my friend. If I could, I would have you come and work for me properly but then you might end up taking my job so maybe it's not such a good idea. No, the reason we are laughing is because Jordi and his partner Toni are with me in my office and we were just talking about this case. There is a little problem at the moment. What we know is that a bank account was set up about six months ago with Sabadell Bank in a branch in the city of Vigo in Galicia in the name Gabriel Hernandez. Large sums of money have been deposited from this company HomeAway but the money has then been transferred to numerous other accounts online but we have frozen this account as of a week ago. We have CCTV still images of a man who set up this account but this man is of North African origin and we have no-one in our system of the name that was used. The passport and utility bills that were used to set up the account are forgeries. We have followed the money, quite large sums, and we know that some of it has been withdrawn from several accounts in Mallorca, including Sóller. The people making the withdrawals have been caught on camera but have been wearing hats or hoodies. We think one of them might be your Fornalutx guy. The mobile phone is 'pay as you go' and has been inactive for ten days but we know it had previously been used in the Fornalutx area.

"The HomeAway account for the property and several others linked to the same account were set up using an IP address based in Vigo. Jordi here has been liaising with police in Vigo and simultaneous searches were planned for three addresses in Vigo, one in Sóller, and your guy's place in Fornalutx. We think there are a group of them all working together. Jordi is planning to seize cash, documents, mobile phones, computer hard drives, bank cards; all the usual stuff. The problem is that police in Vigo are right now dealing with a major incident. A cruise liner coming into port has collided with a passenger ferry and there have been several fatalities. We will only know later tonight if they can release the manpower for the searches in the morning, but if not tomorrow, we hope it will be on Wednesday," said Ramon.

"Well it sounds like you and Jordi have it all in hand. I knew you would but you know me Ramon, I am eager to get on with things. Tell Jordi, if there is anything I can do to help, just ring me. I have given him my number," said James.

"I will tell him James, of course. Thanks for the call and I'll get Jordi to ring you after the operation is complete. Okay amigo?"

"Thanks Ramon, as usual. Good luck. Adiós."

James came off the phone feeling less disgruntled than at the start of the call. He felt he should never have doubted that Jordi would have been working expeditiously to bring the case to a satisfactory conclusion. He was now feeling that its conclusion was imminent and returned to the shop to purchase his ingredients.

The following morning James was getting ready before serving breakfast at Hotel Artesa and was taking an early morning shower, when Charlotte walked into the bathroom and sleepily handed James his mobile phone saying,

"It's someone called Jordi who works with Ramon."

"Yes Jordi, James here," he said, putting the phone to his ear.

"I am sorry to bother you so early James but we are at this guy Enrique's flat in Fornalutx. We have found a lot of cash and other items of evidence but he is not here. Do you know where he might be? Any friends or a girlfriend maybe?" he asked.

"Let me think," said James, drying himself with a towel with one hand. "The only guy I know who knows him for sure is a friend of mine who lives in Sóller. I don't think he would be involved but I don't know exactly where he lives. His name is Ricardo and he works in the ironmonger's here in the village. I know his flat is somewhere near the carpark called Calatrava in Sóller. That's not where your other search was, was it?" asked James.

"No, it was in a street called Carrer Isabel Segundo," replied Jordi.

"Right. Let me ring my friend to see if he knows anything. I will do it in a way so that he doesn't suspect anything and I will ring you back. Vale?"

"Vale. Gracias."

James wrapped a towel around himself and dialled Ricardo's number. It went to voicemail so he hung up, rather than leave a message as to why he was ringing him at just after seven o'clock on a Tuesday morning. He was about to dial Jordi's number to inform him when an in-coming call from Ricardo lit up the screen of his mobile phone.

"Hello. Ricardo?" asked James.

There was a short pause and then James could hear someone yawning on the other end of the phone.

"Oh my God, is that the time? James why did you ring me so early?" asked the familiar voice of Ricardo.

"Have a late night did you?" enquired James.

"I got in about four o'clock. I was at Bar Nadal in Sóller and it is my day off today and I was planning to sleep late but I saw your missed call. Is it about football?" asked Ricardo, yawning loudly into the phone.

"Yeah, sorry. I need to make sure we have got fourteen players for tomorrow night as we will need to pay for the floodlights as well as the pitch and I don't want to book the pitch until I know everyone can make it, and I'm going to be busy at the hotel all day today, so…"

"Yeah, yeah. I will play," replied Ricardo.

"Sounds like a good night. Anyone else there I know?" asked James, hoping to garner any useful information, without drawing attention to his interrogation.

"Oh, just Andreu, Enrique, Paula, Biel, and a few others."

"By the way, I tried to get that photo from your mate Enrique but his phone just kept going to voicemail. Has he changed his number or anything?" asked James.

"I don't know and I don't care. The guy is a psycho! I don't want to have anything more to do with him. He split my lip open last night when he punched me. I still don't know why he did it. I told you he was loco," said Ricardo.

"Do you know where he is now?" asked James, getting to the point, given that Ricardo appeared to have fallen out with Enrique.

"I don't know where that 'cabrón' is! The last I saw, he was walking out of Bar Nadal with his arm around Magdalena's daughter probably going to her place."

"Do you mean Magdalena, who works in the Spar in Fornalutx? Her daughter Aina?" asked James.

"Yes, I think her name is Aina. Why are you so interested in Enrique, James?" asked a curious Ricardo.

"I'll tell you later. I've got to go. Gracias, hombre."

James came off the phone and got dressed quickly, while pondering his next move. He could just ring Jordi back and tell him that he thought his suspect was in a flat above the pharmacy overlooking Plaça d'Espanya in Fornalutx, as he knew that was where Aina lived. He stopped himself from doing that, in deference to Magdalena, Aina's mother. She was a lovely lady and would be working hard at the Spar literally feet from her daughter's flat and the last thing James wanted was for her to have the shame of her daughter's flat being raided by police and a suspect arrested within. *There had to be another way,* he thought.

James, in his previous career as a police officer, had learned that 'a result' was desirable but not at any price. To be a good police officer you needed to understand and respect the needs of the local community whom you served. Tact and diplomacy were useful attributes and he had fostered these tools, especially in sensitive areas of Belfast like the Ardoyne, where police and community relations were quite often strained.

James walked into Hotel Artesa and asked Monica, his assistant, to start serving breakfast without him. He then walked down the steps to the plaça and he could see that the shutters of Aina's flat were pulled shut. He glanced over at the entrance to the Spar mini market and could see Magdalena behind the counter just inside the entrance diligently serving a customer. The plaça was still fairly quiet with just a couple of locals sipping coffee outside Bar Deportivo and Café sa Plaça. There was no way of telling if Enrique was actually inside or not, and if he told Jordi his suspicions he couldn't be sure Jordi would be as tactful as James would want and he may go in, regardless of the knock-on effect any arrest at Aina's may have on her and her mother. He knew that Enrique owned a scooter: it was a cream and green Lambretta. James walked a few yards further down the street to a motos parking bay to find that his scooter was parked there. He knew that Enrique normally parked it outside his flat further down the village, so this gave further credence to him being in Aina's flat. He decided to take the risk and rang Jordi to let him know what he had discovered.

"Jordi. It's James. I think I know where Enrique is. Can you come to the motos bay opposite Inmobiliaria Calabri, towards the plaça?" he asked.

"Sure, we will come now."

"Actually Jordi, can you just come with maybe another plain-clothes officer?"

"No problem."

A few minutes later James was joined by Jordi and his colleague.

"So where do you think he is?" asked Jordi.

"This scooter here is Enrique's. Normally it would be parked outside his own flat but I think he spent the night, and is still in a flat, above the pharmacy belonging to a girl called Aina. I know her mum and she's working in the Spar at the moment. Rather than you guys going in 'all guns blazing', would you be prepared to wait until he comes outside?" asked James, hopefully.

"Okay, but we can't just sit here and wait all day," said Jordi.

"I appreciate that but give me a minute to see if I can do this without involving Aina, will you?" asked James.

"¡Vale, vale, venga!" said Jordi, motioning to James with his hands to get on with it.

James walked back up to the plaça and to the main communal door that led to Aina's flat and rang the buzzer to her flat on the intercom system and waited. There was no reply so he buzzed again. After a few seconds he could hear a crackling noise coming from the speaker of the intercom and then heard a female voice say,

"Sí.¿Que fas?"

"Hola Aina, es James.¿Enrique es allí?" asked James.

"Sí.¿Por que?" she asked.

"Un hombre es el robo de su moto. ¡Venga!" said James, pretending someone was stealing Enrique's moped.

"Oh vale, vale."

James waited for a few minutes on the corner of the plaça, a few feet from the communal wooden door to the three apartments and could see Jordi and the other officer about fifty metres further down the street by the motos bay. He could hear the sound of footsteps descending stairs and then saw the wooden door open and Enrique started walking towards him, putting on his brown leather jacket.

"¿Que pasa?" he asked hurriedly of James.

"¡Prisa! Su moto," said James to him, pointing towards the motos bay, where his scooter was parked.

James had expected Jordi and his colleague to wait out of sight, as despite the fact they were casually dressed, their demeanour obviously made Enrique nervous, as before he reached the bay, Enrique turned and started running back the way he had come, away from the two officers, who had made little or no effort to look inconspicuous. Enrique was almost back to James and he was now being chased by the two officers who were shouting for him to stop. James sighed with indignation because it hadn't gone the way it should have and because he felt the blame did not lie with him and also because of what he felt he now had to do. There was no point in blocking Enrique's path or gesturing for him to stop. Previous experience had taught James that in order not to get hurt yourself and in order for you, or in this case others, to affect an arrest you couldn't muck about. James leapt at the torso of the encroaching Enrique akin to a high rugby tackle, pushing him backwards and he landed firmly on his back with a thud with James' full weight bearing down on him. The two officers were upon them instantaneously, before Enrique had a chance to struggle but with the look of surprise that was evident on Enrique's face James thought he wouldn't have put up much of a struggle in any case. Jordi quickly and nimbly turned the prisoner onto his front and placed a set of 'quick cuffs' on him. Both officers then lifted him to his feet and started marching him unceremoniously down the street in the direction of his flat. James had by now picked himself up off the pavement and watched as they led Enrique away without a word from him. Jordi briefly looked back and gave James a 'thumbs up' signal and he reciprocated with a wave.

James took no pleasure in intervening, especially when so close to his home but he felt the actions of the officers left him with no choice. Just then, Simon, the owner of Café Med, approached him from behind with his arms full of baguettes.

"What was that all about?" he asked with incredulity.

"Oh, nothing really Simon," said James calmly.

"It's nothing to do with...you know?" he asked animatedly.

"Oh no, no. That's all done and dusted," said James, realising that Simon was referring to James' near miss with a London gangster, Danny Kusemi, several years previously.

"Never a dull moment in Fornalutx," laughed Simon, as he headed towards his restaurant.

"Never a dull moment is right," said James quietly to himself, as he turned and made his way back to his hotel for the start of another working day.

Chapter 10

Rehab for the Soul

James looked at the industrial-sized wall clock in the 'entrada' of Hotel Artesa. It was now almost half past five. It was the third occasion he had checked the time within the last hour. Time seemed to be passing exceptionally slowly. Most of his guests were out of the hotel and enjoying the warm autumnal sunshine of the mid-October Friday. He knew that six of his guests were out on a long walk through the Tramuntana Mountains and had left shortly after breakfast. They had a walk of approximately twenty-eight kilometres planned and had left the hotel shortly after ten o'clock, so he didn't expect to see them much before he finished work at six o'clock. They were planning on walking from Fornalutx along part of the GR221, or dry stone wall route, into the mountains to Cúber reservoir. James had tackled this walk during the previous spring and had enjoyed the open mountain scenery, following the paths through the Ofre estate. On that occasion, he and his walking group had been lucky enough to catch a glimpse of a

Black Vulture circling overhead. Once at Cúber reservoir, they made a detour to the summit of Puig de l'Ofre, a mountain of just over a thousand metres and their efforts were rewarded with the most spectacular panoramic views. He saw the Bay of Palma, as well as the Bay of Alcúdia and the east of the island. With a pair of binoculars, he could even see the Castle of Alaró perched at the top of the Puig d'Alaró.

This was not why James kept checking the time. He was eager to finish because he was going to be spending the weekend on his houseboat in Palma with his family. He was aware that both of his sons had finished school and were next door in his house. Charlotte had been to the supermarket to get a few provisions for their two-night stay and although James tended to go to Palma on a regular basis doing the school run, he was really looking forward to staying on his houseboat for only the third time since he had acquired it. It was the first time for several months that both he and Charlotte had arranged to have cover, so they could have two full days off together. Monica would be in charge at Hotel Artesa and her sister would be helping her for the duration of their short break. He had booked the weekend on the houseboat for their own use, as the remainder of the time James allowed police associations to send officers suffering from Post-Traumatic Stress Disorder or physical injuries sustained on duty, to escape there for much-needed rest and recuperation.

Six o'clock finally arrived after James had spoken to Monica. There were to be no guest arrivals or departures over the next couple of days, so things at the hotel should run straightforwardly. He returned home, changed into more casual attire and then Charlotte, he and his boys set off with their weekend bags to their car and drove the thirty or so kilometres to the marina in Palma.

They spent the first evening enjoying the privileged views that the spacious deck of the boat provided and James was in his element grilling on the gas barbeque. After dinner, he and the boys had some father and son time doing a spot of fishing off the bow of the boat but darkness soon descended without them having caught anything. Undaunted, they embarked on a family game of Monopoly at the table in the cosy open-plan living area of the boat. Although the boat had Wi-Fi, James felt that it was good for his sons to spend some time away from the internet, X-boxes and Minecraft and it was quality family time.

The following morning, he woke early and thought it would be lovely to enjoy a lie-in and relax in the compact but luxuriously equipped double bedroom in the bow of the boat. However, he had gone to the trouble of bringing his running gear with him and he thought that a gentle jog along the wide promenade of the Paseo Marítimo should be taken advantage of. Charlotte was still asleep but he could hear his sons chatting in the small bedroom next door. He dressed for his run and grabbed his ubiquitous iPod and headphones and set off along the jetty. He turned right along the Paseo Marítimo and headed towards La Seu, Palma's majestic gothic cathedral.

James felt very relaxed and decided to run at a slower pace than he did when he ran around Fornalutx. With the purpose-built wide pedestrian and cycle paths right along the seafront, it made running a more pleasant and less dangerous enterprise, than avoiding cars on the roads in and around his village. It was a beautiful October morning and the capital was just waking up to a leisurely weekend for most. It was not even half past seven but James was surprised by the number of joggers along his route. Traffic was passing on his left, and to his right he could see the large number of yachts and super yachts moored in the various marina areas from Club del Mar round to Real Club Náutico. Ahead he could see the dominating and impressive sandstone façade of the thirteenth-century Cathedral of Santa Maria with its forty-four metre tall nave and buttresses dominating the skyline. What made it all the more impressive for James, as he got ever closer to it, was its location overlooking the old harbour. Beside it was the thirteenth-century Royal Palace of Almudaina, originally an Arabian fort before it became an official royal residence but more recently it was used for state receptions and other ceremonies. James recalled his own ceremony three years previously when he had been presented with his medal. That day the striking architecture of the building and its interior would always hold special memories for him.

He continued his steady pace past both buildings until he came level with a favourite play park of Reuben's beside the Parc de la Mar, located on the other side of the carriageways, and stopped. He looked all around him and removed his headphones and switched off his iPod. He took a few seconds to really appreciate that he was standing in the middle of a most beautiful city, overlooking the sea and the Playa de Palma on an island which he now called home. At that moment, he realised just how fortunate he was. Things could have been so very different for him. He realised this more than he let on and tried not to dwell on how previous incidents with Danny Kusemi and the Serbian hitman, 'Ale Boris', could have turned out.

James was not an overtly emotional man; something that Charlotte had tried, without great success, to change. For James, it wasn't that he didn't have feelings and emotions, and it wasn't as Charlotte sometimes accused him, of seeing it as a form of weakness to display emotion. James rather felt that it was better to remain on an even keel and not display too much of either happiness or sadness. Perhaps it was because he had had enough traumatic experiences in twelve short years of policing for anyone's life, coupled with the more recent incidents, especially the kidnapping of his son Adam that had made him phlegmatic.

This weekend was already proving to be great medicine for him and he understood why he had received so many e-mails of gratitude from the numerous police officers who had stayed on *Soul*, his houseboat. It was in such a privileged location and the delights and charms of the boat and the city were there in abundance for all to see. He couldn't quite fathom how the majority of tourists who arrived on the island on package holidays would only see Palma from the window of a plane or from a coach going to and from the airport. Perhaps it was better that they didn't all know what they were missing, as he thought Palma in the height of the summer could be quite a crowded place.

James returned his headphones to his ears and switched on his iPod once again and resumed his exercise, returning in the direction of his houseboat. On his return, Charlotte and his sons were having breakfast on deck.

"Good morning! Good morning! Permission to come aboard Cap'n?" asked James, with a wonky salute to anyone who would acknowledge his attempt at humour.

Both his sons looked around at him and then at each other before Adam said,

"Look at Dad, Reuben. He thinks this is a real boat you know but it hasn't even got an engine."

"That doesn't matter, it is still a boat. Rowing boats and some sailing boats don't have engines but they might still have a captain. So, yeah Reuben, look at Dad," said James, mimicking his son Adam.

"Daaad! I didn't say it like that. Anyway, this boat doesn't have a captain, so there," said Adam dogmatically.

"Alright, alright your ladyship! Keep your wig on!" said James, waiting for a reaction.

"Muuuum!" cried Adam, looking for support.

"You are worse than the children," scolded Charlotte, joining the boys at the table with a cup of coffee.

"I'm only kidding wee man. Anyway, this boat does have a captain: me. What's that famous poem by Walt Whitman? 'Oh, Captain! My Captain!' or maybe I'm thinking of a *Carry On* film; Ooooh Captain! Oh my, Captain!" said James, attempting his best Kenneth Williams impersonation.

"What?" Adam asked. Reuben shook his head.

"Anyway, what a beautiful morning! I've just done my exercise for the day. What about you guys? What exercise are you going to do today?" asked James.

"I thought we were coming here from some relaxation," said Adam indignantly.

"We are," interjected Charlotte. "We can do something active and have fun at the same time you know."

"Like what?" Reuben asked.

"Why don't we hire bikes and ride them along the bike path and go around to Portixol and around there?" proposed James.

"Yeah and we can stop and have lunch in that beach bar in s'Arenal with the surf boards. You know, the one you liked Adam when you did the kite surfing course?" said Charlotte enthusiastically, trying to make it sound fun.

"Oh yeah, I remember that place. It did really good ribs. Yeah, that's not a bad idea," agreed Adam.

"How far will I have to ride?" asked Reuben.

James looked at Charlotte and mouthed "Are you sure?" realising that the round trip could be nearly thirty kilometres and that Reuben was known for getting tired quite easily, when it suited him.

"Oh, not that far," said Charlotte, "We can do a little bit at a time. We can just take our time, and Reuben, we can make a list of, say, ten things and the first person to see all ten wins a prize; a sort of treasure hunt, yeah?"

"Okay, that sounds like fun," said Reuben, nodding.

The four enjoyed the morning and early afternoon gently cycling on the cycle path along the promenade of the Playa de Palma, relaxing over a pleasant lunch. The return journey was managed by Reuben without complaint as he was kept active in his pursuit of finding items to see, ranging from skateboarders to someone walking more than one dog. All items on the list of ten were found first somewhat fortuitously by Reuben, whose prize was a new white peaked cap with an anchor and the word 'Captain' emblazoned on the front.

The bikes were returned to the rental shop and a well-earned siesta was taken by James and Charlotte back on the houseboat, while the boys were allowed an hour of game time on the iPad. James had arranged for the family to meet up with their friends, Tim and Sue and their daughter Sarah, who now lived in Bendinat, on the outskirts of Palma. Sarah and Reuben were of a similar age and had known each other for several years during the time when their friends lived in Sóller. Adam had arranged to meet up with some school friends from his international school and they were going to see a film in English at the cinema in nearby Porto Pi.

"Permission to come aboard?" came the recognisable voice of Tim, as James quickly grabbed Reuben's new captain's hat and tried to put it on, only to realise it was about five sizes too small.

"Aye, permission granted, me hearties!" said James, attempting a gruff pirate voice, whilst holding the under-sized hat on top of his head.

Drawing a smile from both Tim and Sue, all three came onto the deck and greeted James.

"This is pretty spectacular, old boy!" said Tim, looking around him.

"Wow, James! This is lovely! You know we have been dying to get to see this for so long," said Sue.

"I know, I know. We should have had you here long before now but we don't really get to use it ourselves very often. Now, who's for a G & T?"

"You don't even need to ask old boy. Sounds good to me," said Tim, wandering below deck to see more.

"Is Charlotte down below James?" asked Sue.

"Yeah, she's just getting ready. Go and have a look and I'll bring your drinks down to you. Sarah, Reuben's down below if you want to go too?" asked James.

James joined all five who were chatting in the open-plan living-dining area of the houseboat. James brought drinks for all and sat down with his family and friends.

"This is really great James. I love the encaustic tiles you've used and the panelling. You must be very happy with it?" asked Sue.

"Yeah, it's great and I know that our guests who use it are pretty appreciative," said James, handing round the drinks.

"Well, it's lovely to see you all, so salud!" he said, clinking glasses.

"¡Salud! ¡Salud! Cheers!"

"Yes, very honourable of you, old boy, to allow your old colleagues to use it for free. There wouldn't be any chance of a weekend for a stressed out architect and his trouble and strife, would there?" asked Tim, grinning.

"Oh I'm sure we might be able to fit you in for a small fee," said James, smiling.

"Where are we going this evening by the way?" asked Charlotte.

"It's a surprise. You'll have to wait and see," replied James. "Adam has arranged to stay overnight with his friend Luke, and Luke's dad will drop him back in the morning, so we don't need to be back here for any particular time. Obviously within reason because of this pair of hooligans," said James, nodding towards the wives.

"Will we be partaking in one or two libations this evening m'lud?" asked Tim.

"One or two. Well, I'm ready when you are," said James, finishing his gin and tonic.

"What's the rush? He can't relax, this one. He's always looking at his watch. Tranquilo." said Charlotte.

James waited while the others finished their drinks and then they set off walking towards Passeig del Born and the area known as La Lonja, named after the former maritime trade exchange. James led the way, walking through the atmospheric Plaça de la Drassana and along the narrow, cobbled streets full of restaurants, bars and clubs until he came to their first port of call, Abaco Bar.

James stood outside on arrival and said,

"I've never been in here and I have heard it's a bit whacky so I thought, why not?"

"Okay. We were here one night a long time ago with Pete and Vicky. They do the most amazing cocktails but they come at a price," said Sue.

"And before you ask, they do non-alcoholic cocktails so the kids can have one as well," said James, before opening an unassuming wooden door into a large courtyard of an old palatial house, full of over-the-top theatrical opulence and grandeur. Loud classical music filled the air and the covered terrace with its segmental arches and Tuscan columns were only upstaged by the abundant displays of flowers and fruit, bird cages and fountains. Inside the nobleman's house itself, it was as if the owners had just stepped out and James felt like he had been transported back by about a hundred and fifty years.

After an initial tour of the various rooms and courtyard area, all six returned and sat down in the amazing courtyard, where a plethora of formally dressed waiters were eager to take their order.

"This place can't help but make you smile," said James, looking all around him and marvelling at the architecture and the sheer gaudiness of some of the additions and props. "It's certainly unique, that's for sure."

After a round of refreshing, albeit expensive cocktails, which James felt were worth every cent just to be able to drink in such grandiose surroundings, he led the party back out into the narrow streets, flanked by tall, narrow townhouses, now mostly split into apartments. They didn't have far to go to the restaurant that James had booked a week earlier, just to make sure of getting a table at the renowned restaurant Forn de Sant Joan.

The two families were shown to their table and given menus. Silence descended and it was all heads down as everyone scanned the menu. James was the first to break the silence.

"This is my kind of food. I could have anything on here and I don't think I would be disappointed. It all looks delicious. Decisions, decisions," he said, beckoning a waiter. "Drinks people. Shall I get some water for the kids and shall I get a bottle of red and a white too?"

"That's fine, James. You choose. I'm sure anything will be good," replied Tim.

"Vale. Una botella grande de agua sin gas, una botella de Ses Nines vino tinto y una botella de Macià Batle vino blanco por favour. Es todo," said James to the waiter.

"Muy bien, señor," he replied.

"Reuben, what about some tapas for you? They look really nice, they have a selection on that table behind you," said Charlotte.

"Awe mum, can't I have some fish or something? I'm really hungry you know," said Reuben pleadingly, as he continued to scan the menu.

"This kid eats better than I do," laughed James. "Okay then buddy, that's fine. What about grilled sea bass, sautéed spinach with garlic and creamy parmesan sauce?"

"Mmm! That sounds good. Yes, can I have that please?" asked Reuben.

"So, you're not a chicken nuggets and fries man then Reuben?" asked Tim, smiling.

"It's alright, I guess," said Reuben, shrugging his shoulders.

"Good man! You stick to the expensive sea bass. Your dad is paying for the whole bill," laughed Tim.

The waiter returned with the wine and water and removed the cork from the white wine bottle and asked James if he would like to taste it but he directed him to Charlotte before the waiter did the same with the red wine, which James just asked him to pour.

"This is a bit like *The Emperor's New Clothes*," started James.

"What is?" asked Sue, looking perplexed.

"Tasting wine before the waiter pours you a glass. In nearly thirty years of drinking wine, I have never sent a bottle back for being corked. I'm not even sure if I would know what a bottle of corked wine tastes like. I know he didn't do it there but quite often the waiter will show you the label and they still go through the tasting nonsense, even if it is from a screw top bottle, in which case it can't be corked. We, not wishing to offend, go through with the charade. A bit like *The Emperor's New Clothes*."

"I suppose you're right. This red is quite a cheeky little number. I'm getting vanilla pods, blackcurrant, sweaty socks and wet dog," said Tim, swilling his wine glass under his nose and inhaling loudly before taking a mouthful and making loud slurping sounds in a mockery of wine experts.

"Daddy! Stop misbehaving!" said Sarah, his daughter.

"Sorry Poppet. Daddy won't misbehave for at least the next five minutes. It really speaks volumes when you are told off by your nine year old," laughed Tim.

"Well, I don't know about you guys but I'm starving," said Charlotte.

The waiter returned to the table with his notepad and pen at the ready.

"I'd like the monkfish with sautéed vegetables and Café de Paris sauce, and the grilled sea bass para el niño," said Charlotte, getting the ball rolling.

"Is no-one having a starter?" asked Sue.

"I want to leave some room for dessert," said Charlotte.

James shook his head.

"Okay then, I'll have the grilled venison steak, polenta with nuts, fig carpaccio and rosemary-honey sauce. I'd like that cooked medium por favor, and Sarah, what are you having? Would you like some croquetas?" asked Sue.

"I want what Reuben's having," said Sarah, in a matter-of- fact way.

"Okay," said Sue, sighing. "You'll never finish it but anyway. Un autro labina a la plancha."

"Vale.¿Y los señores?" asked the waiter.

"I'll have the roast suckling pig, apple compote and apples stuffed with kefir. If you've run out of non-believers, you can get the chef to stuff the apples with someone else. I'm not fussy either way," said Tim, looking very pleased with himself.

"I think you will find that is 'kafir' sir. Kefir is a type of milk fermented with kefir grains," said the waiter in unbroken English, to everyone's surprise.

"Stone the crows! Are you an Englishman old bean?" asked Tim.

"My father is Mallorcan, my mother is English but I was born in Mallorca. You might know my uncle and my cousin. Do you like rugby?" asked the waiter.

"Which self-respecting Englishman doesn't? Never worry about the 'bog trotter' there, his lot have fallen behind lately," quipped Tim.

"Do you know Owen Farrell, who plays for England and his dad Andy, who was the coach?"

"And you are related to them? Well done you. What's your name amigo?" asked Tim.

"It's Guillem. And for you, sir?" he asked, turning to James.

"I'd like the beef tenderloin, and medium please. Thanks, Guillem," said James, handing him his menu.

Guillem left to process the order.

"So our mate Guillem here is related to the Farrell's then? You wouldn't have expected that in Palma, would you? They are both Northerners, who went from league to union. That reminds me; I once had to do plans for the northern owner of JB Sports before he sold it for God knows how many millions. He was a right 'northern lad', salt of the earth type," said Tim, putting on a strong generic northern English accent. "So, he rings me up and he says 'Tim, what the fuck's wrong with these plans? They're not what I asked for. You'll have to fly up to Leeds and sort this out. I'm not fucking havin' this.' So he sends his helicopter for me in Hertfordshire and his pilot takes me back to Leeds. I think it was late on a Friday and I get to his office and he had been looking at the plans upside down so he just went, 'Ah well, you can fuck off then.' So, his pilot dropped me back home at a cost of probably about ten grand or something. Unbelievable!"

"Daddy, you're misbehaving again, saying bad words!" said Sarah, reprimanding her father.

"I'm not swearing Poppet. That's just how all Northern people speak," replied Tim, in a tongue-in-cheek manner.

The food arrived and everyone enjoyed the remainder of their evening but when both kids started to yawn, it was decided to call time and both families headed to their respective houses and houseboats, glad to have caught up and enjoyed each other's company.

After a lazy Sunday relaxing on the houseboat, James and his family returned to Fornalutx in the evening, refreshed and invigorated. He realised that although they lived in a beautiful village and ran a great business, which they enjoyed doing, it was nonetheless important to take time out and spend some quality time with friends and family, away from their home or workplace environment and he resolved to do it more often.

Chapter 11

All Hands on Deck

James removed his headphones and dried the sweat from his face and head with his towel. He lifted his drinks bottle from the holder on the running machine and gulped down the remainder of his water. He had finished his usual work-out of a mixture of weight-training and cardiovascular exercise at the gym and walked towards the exit door. Xavi, the gym supervisor smiled at James in his usual, friendly way, tinged with what James suspected was a mixture of respect and amusement. James was in his late forties and was a regular at the gymnasium and had come to know most of the staff and the other regular members, if not by name, at least he was on speaking or nodding terms with them. He was one of the older members but he felt sure that he would win the award for the person most resembling someone who had completed a marathon, for at the end of each session he would be soaked in sweat and glowing red. Some of the younger members hardly seemed to break sweat.

"Adéu. ¡Necisito una ducha de agua fria! ¡Poc a poc!" said James, referring to his need for a cold shower and that it was necessary to take working out bit by bit, mixing Spanish and the little Catalan he knew.

"Poc a poc. Sí, sí, sí. Adéu," replied Xavi, laughing at James' attempt at Catalan but agreeing with his sentiment.

James went to his locker and retrieved his rucksack and walked to the changing room. He sat down on the wooden bench and removed his moist gym clothes and then took a shower. He dried himself and got dressed, having to reapply the towel to his head and face, even though he had stopped exercising almost ten minutes earlier. He descended the stairs and walked outside into the cool November evening and instantaneously enjoyed the cool breeze. As he walked towards his car in the car park, he unzipped a pocket in his rucksack and retrieved his mobile phone and noticed he had a missed call about an hour earlier from Ramon. He threw his rucksack onto the front passenger seat of his car, got into the driver's seat and rang Ramon. The ringing tone was immediately picked up by his Bluetooth in-car system on the car speakers.

"Hey Ramon, what's up? I'm just returning your call," said James.

"Hi James, I just thought you should know, we expect the container ship from Cartagena to arrive in Palma early tomorrow morning. I thought it would be courteous to keep you informed rather than tell you when it was all over. After all, it was due to your initial accident that has made this possible. We are all set here in Palma and my guys are ready at the other premises near you, so wish us luck amigo. This is a big operation for me," said Ramon.

"It will be fine Ramon. I know you have been working hard on this and it will certainly boost your annual drugs seizure quota, I have no doubt about that. I suppose you have to assume everyone involved will be armed?" asked James.

"The risk assessment on this is about ten pages long! We have two tactical support teams in place as well as my own men and I will be at the docks myself from early tomorrow morning," replied Ramon.

"Listen, thanks for thinking of me and I hope you get a result but be safe."

"Thanks, amigo. We can have a drink to celebrate when it is all over but for now adiós. Buenas noches."

"Buenas noches y suerte," said James, hanging up.

James sat for a moment, feeling enamoured that Ramon had taken the trouble to inform him of the latest development at a potentially crucial and sensitive time in his police operation. He felt honoured in the trust that had been conveyed by the phone call. This feeling was superseded by one of apprehension that everything would go well for Ramon and his officers and that they would make arrests, confiscate the drug haul and have enough evidence to prosecute all those involved.

Well, there's nothing I can do to help, he thought, as he started his car and drove back to Fornalutx.

He drove past the plaça, which was deserted. Café sa Plaça and Bar Deportivo were closed but he could see the lights of Bar Ca'n Benet still on. It was usual for the other two bars to keep less regular hours at this time of year. Ca'n Benet remained open all year and was usually full of locals, especially when Barcelona or Real Madrid were playing football and James remembered that both teams were playing each other that night in a league game. He parked his car and walked the short distance to the bar and stepped inside. There were about twenty village residents inside, all glued to the large flat screen television on the wall and a few other couples, including an English couple who were staying at his hotel.

"Good evening. Will you be watching the football when it starts?" he asked.

"Oh, hi there. We are just soaking up the atmosphere, we didn't even know there was a game on. Who's playing?" asked his male guest.

"It's a big game tonight. Barca against Real Madrid. They are both well-supported around here. In fact, I would say support in this bar is about fifty- fifty, so it's always a spectacle just watching the local punters and the verbal abuse and banter that goes with it. Can I get you a drink?" asked James.

"No thanks. We're fine. Enjoy the game though."

"Thanks. See you at breakfast," said James approaching the bar.

"Hola, que tal. Dígame," said Josep, one of the barmen.

"Una Estrella Galicia por favor."

"Vale, James."

James received his bottle of beer and took a refreshing sip and turned around as someone had asked for the volume of the television to be turned up, so he realised that the match was ready to start. Just then he saw his friend and one of his tennis and football partners, Danut, a Romanian who lived in the village.

Danut saw him from his seat at a table with several other villagers and waved him over to join them, nearer to the television. James started walking to the vacant chair at Danut's table, squeezing past several villagers, some of whom he greeted and was just about to take a seat. He stopped and glanced down towards the back of the bar, which was dimly lit and he quickly moved down his prescription glasses, which were on top of his head. Clarity of vision was instantly restored and James' heart missed a beat, for sitting at the end table in the bar was Jimmy Knox. He was sitting in the company of two other men who had their backs to James. He sat down quickly but continued to look at Knox, who didn't appear to have seen him. James gently manoeuvred his chair into a position where he could lean over and see Knox, whilst using Danut as a screen.

"Everything okay James?" asked Danut, looking over his shoulder in the direction of James' gaze.

"Yeah, yeah. It's fine Danut but do me a favour and don't look around at those guys," said James nervously.

He felt very uncomfortable and sitting in his current position was just too precarious and vulnerable for his liking. *What the hell was Knox doing back in Mallorca and in his local bar? Who were the two men with him and were they being watched by Ramon's guys?* he asked himself.

"I have to go Danut. I'll see you later," said James, getting up from his seat and walking quickly outside with his beer bottle.

He closed the door behind him and walked to the window of the bar and peeked between some event posters stuck to the window. He could still see Knox at the table but he couldn't get a good look at his companions, other than to see that they were both male and had short dark hair. From the build of one of them, James guessed that he was a body-builder. He scanned the remainder of the bar for any sign of undercover police. He could identify the majority as being regulars of the bar. The English couple had left and there was now only another couple, who from their height, their blonde hair and blue eyes, he felt that they were odds-on to be Swedish or German. Unless the bar was being watched from nearby, it didn't appear that any close surveillance was in operation.

He couldn't understand what Knox was doing back there. It had to be because of the imminent landing of the drug shipment. The only conclusion about Knox that he could formulate, was that he had either been forced to return and act as a lackey, or worse still, that he had come voluntarily and was either stupid enough to think he could still be involved without risk, or was reckless enough to think that his reward would be worth a prison sentence. James didn't have the answers but he needed to make Ramon aware of the situation and fast.

He pulled his mobile phone from his pocket and rang Ramon's number as he walked towards the small water fountain at the edge of the plaça. It was now nearly a quarter past ten.

"Hola James, I wasn't expecting to hear from you again tonight. What is it?"

"Ramon," started James, trying to talk softly, "I am outside Bar Ca'n Benet in the plaça in Fornalutx and Jimmy Knox is inside drinking with another two men!"

"What? Are you kidding me? What the fuck is he doing there?" said Ramon, clearly surprised by the revelation.

"So you didn't know he was here? I wasn't sure if your team was watching him or not. I can't get a proper look at the other two as I don't want Knox to see me. It might scupper your whole operation," said James, with a degree of urgency.

"No, no, you must not, I repeat must not go back inside. Are you sure Knox didn't see you James?" asked an equally animated Ramon.

"As sure as I can be. I thought you or the NCA were continuing to keep tabs on him?" asked James.

"My understanding was that the NCA had monitored his movements for a week after he returned from here and were satisfied that he was a bit-part player and didn't have the resources to monitor him around the clock. I was assured that there was an alert on his movements if he left the UK, so either that was never done or he has managed to enter the island undetected. James, I need to ring my guys watching the olivar. They are the closest to you. I need someone there now. Can you safely watch their position without being seen until I get one of my guys there?" asked Ramon.

"Yes, you can count on it," replied James.

"I will get at least one of my guys to do a 'walk past' and make sure they pick up the targets. I need to know who the other two men are who are with Knox. Pick a place where my guys can safely meet you in ten minutes."

"Okay. Let me think. Get them to meet me outside the Banco Popular here in the village. I can see if Knox and his cohorts leave from there and it is out of view from where they are at present," said James, beginning to walk to the meeting point.

"Vale, vale. Ring me once you have spoken with my guys. Adiós."

James walked back past the bar and glanced inside as he did so and he could see that Knox was now at the bar but his two companions were still seated at the table to the rear. He walked around the corner and continued until he reached the Banco Popular and waited. He walked back and forth a few feet in order to cover both potential exit routes from the bar should Knox leave. A few minutes later, James could hear the sound of a car driving into Fornalutx, coming from the direction of Biniaraix and Sóller. The car pulled over beside him and he could see there were two men inside. They switched off the lights and the engine. The driver rolled down the window.

"Buenas noches.¿Coma te llamas?" he asked.

"Me llamo James.¿ Hablas inglés?" he asked hopefully.

"Un poco, a little."

"Did Ramon send you?" asked James quietly.

"Yes. Can you get into the car?" asked the officer.

"It is better if you come over here and your colleague stays where he is. Do you see the window on your left, up ahead? That is the back bar of Ca'n Benet and I'm scared that one of the suspects might see me and recognise me," said James, moving further back into the shadows.

The plain-clothes officer got out of the driver's seat and closed the car door gently and walked the few feet to James.

"Juan Mayol. I work with Ramon. We have not met but I know who you are," he said, shaking James by the hand. "Okay, I have seen the custody photograph of this guy Knox. Are you sure it is him?"

"Yes, no question about it. It is him."

"So, he is sitting at the back of the bar near the window?" asked Juan.

"Yes. He's with two other men. Both have got short dark hair. One I think is wearing a dark jacket with a grey hoodie and the other one is wearing a lighter-coloured jacket but you can't miss him, he's very stocky, you know has big muscles?" said James, furtively.

"Okay. We will go from here. Ramon told me you must now go home so please…" said Juan, stretching out his arm as James' queue to leave.

"Fair enough, I'll go," said James, walking back up the quiet alley he had come from. He stopped at the corner and decided to take the set of steps to his street that didn't mean passing the bar, in case Knox might see him, and he then opened the front door to his house, locking it behind him. He ascended the staircase to his first-floor study and immediately rang Ramon.

"Right, your guys are in place now. I hope they don't lose them. Any idea who the other two guys are?" asked James.

"No, not yet. My guys have been instructed to get a photo of them using a telephoto lens on the camera they have, so we'll try and identify them through the NCA. I have checked with my counterpart in the NCA and the alert was placed on Jimmy Knox so evidently he has got into Mallorca either on a false passport or he arrived on a private boat, which probably means so too have his two unknown companions. As far as my teams are concerned, the three guys who were sent here as part of the original landing party are accounted for and they have eyes on them. This is assuming that these guys are involved in this. It would be too much of a coincidence that Knox decided to come back for a short holiday with a couple of mates. He wouldn't risk coming back, knowing that I could invoke a European arrest warrant as and when I decided, and the fact that his passport hasn't been used to get here means he's involved," said Ramon.

"Are you satisfied that the NCA haven't recruited him as an informant and are just not willing to tell you?" asked James.

"I can only go by what my British counterpart tells me but I don't think that is the case. He sounded genuinely surprised and annoyed that Knox was here and he apologised for his budget constraints getting us into this position. No, I think Knox is here because he needs the money and I obviously didn't scare him hard enough. It will give me great pleasure in charging the little sneak," said Ramon, murmuring something additionally to himself under his breath.

"So, what happens now?" asked James.

"All that we can do is wait until morning. My guys will follow Knox and the other two. Hopefully they won't split up, as I have had to take my two off the recon at the olivar, leaving only one watching it. It is my belief that Knox and these guys will probably go back there tonight. They are so close to it. Either way, we will follow them and hopefully I can get some sleep tonight. Tomorrow is going to be a busy day and I don't need any more surprises. I suggest you do the same thing James and please, my friend, it goes without saying, I would appreciate it if you would not go out anywhere else tonight."

"Don't worry Ramon. I'm in for the night. You have enough on your plate without me adding to your worries. Take care and good luck," said James.

"Bona nit, bona nit."

Chapter 12

The Operation

"Everyone is here for the briefing, Comisario," said one of Ramon's officers in Spanish.

"Okay. I will be there presently," he replied.

It was half past six in the morning and Comisario Ramon Martinez of the Unidad de Droga y Crimen Organizado sat at his desk, going over his briefing notes to make sure he had covered all eventualities. There could be no mistakes. This was potentially going to be one of the largest cocaine seizures ever in Spain and it was happening on his watch and he was in charge of the operation. A successful operation would mean further promotion boards would find it hard to overlook this feather in his cap. Failure, in his view, could range from no cocaine found at all to fatalities on his side. He took a long, deep breath, lifted his briefing notes and walked into the briefing room.

"Good morning ladies and gentlemen, let's get on with this. I need you all to be focused this morning. I am aware that the container ship called *APL Columbia* is due to dock in approximately two and a half hours at Palma. As I hope you have already read in your briefing packs, we suspect that up to three containers will be unloaded for Charcoal Imports (Mallorca) Ltd. The container numbers and seal numbers are in your notes. We have a surveillance team in position at the two areas covering the port marked A and B on your map, labelled map one. Communications will be on secure channel nine and in the event of any breakdown in communication, a backup channel, channel three, should be used.

"Surveillance team two is in place at the olivar in Biniaraix and those designated for arrests at that location will note their positions marked A and B on map two. Body armour must be worn at all times. Intelligence suggests that this criminal team have access to firearms and I don't want any casualties, at least not on our side. I will personally be attending the port and I will be directing the operation whilst observing CCTV monitors on the third floor of the Ports Authority building. My call sign is Oscar Charlie. Inspector Coll is in charge of the team going to Biniaraix.

"You have a collection of photographs of the five main targets who we expect to be at one or other scene. Familiarise yourself with these men, people. There may well be others who we have not shown here, so expect the unexpected and be prepared. The main target is photograph one. His name is Anthony or Tony Mason. He is a British citizen and he has previous convictions for drug importation, possession of firearms with intent to endanger life, and various offences relating to violence. Intelligence would suggest that he is both the brains and the brawn in this operation and is also responsible for setting up the two fake businesses here on the island. His charcoal business warehouse at the docks is shown at point C on map one. The name is above the main perimeter gate to the compound. We didn't expect him to be present. Our British colleagues in the National Crime Agency had him on round-the-clock surveillance, so it came as a bit of a shock to them when I informed them that someone matching his description was seen with two other suspects in a bar in Fornalutx until midnight last night. Juan Mayol, from my squad, who has gone back to Biniaraix, was able to take photographs last night and it was confirmed a couple of hours ago that this is Mason.

"He is thirty-five years of age, will use a firearm if necessary and he is a big guy who will put up a fight, so Tasers have been authorised for use but if there is any suggestion of him going for a weapon then the suspect should be neutralised and lethal force should be used. The tactical firearms team here will deploy two snipers at points D and E on the map, so bear this in mind. I do not want anyone getting in the way if a clear shot is required. He has been able to get into Mallorca undetected, so obviously he can get out undetected just as easily. He is currently at the olivar with three of the other suspects, who I will come on to.

"There are three vehicles that we know of being used by the targets. All three are listed in your briefing notes. All three have been tagged with tracking devices and all three are currently stationary. My first surveillance team, call sign Sierra Tango One, will follow any vehicles leaving Biniaraix. Call sign Sierra Tango Three, will be tailing any vehicle used by suspect two, from his address in Marivent.

"Suspect two is Stephen McClean, aged thirty-six and a British citizen. Look at photograph two. He is

Mason's head of operations on the island when he is not overseeing things himself. Again, a nasty bastard who is happy to use a firearm and he has previous convictions for drugs and violence-related offences. He has been going to the warehouse most days over the last six weeks and has been going to the olivar about once a week.

"Target three, we have only just found out about. He has been identified as a Michael Finn, aged twenty-five and also a British citizen; convictions for minor drug offences and assault. Intelligence indicates though that he is trying to make a name for himself within Mason's gang, and we therefore think any initial shooting may come from him when challenged.

"Target four is a James Knox, aged twenty-five and a British citizen. It was Knox's initial arrest about two months ago by chance that brought this whole shipment to our attention. He was a drugs mule, as I understood it, and it appeared he was acting under duress. His task was to recover a sample of the product and return to the UK for some of the other potential targets from Holland and Belgium to test it. Our friends from Interpol suggest that their sources believe there could be anything up to a tonne coming in on these pallets and bags of charcoal. You will see from the briefing notes just exactly what we are looking for. So, street value, we are talking around €200 million. Knox has no previous convictions and was given a chance to cooperate with me. It appears that he has decided not to and has decided to chance his luck. He was one of the three suspects seen in Fornalutx last night; Mason and Finn being the other two. All three are currently at the olivar with a cook and I don't mean one who will be making their breakfast. I would doubt that Knox will be armed but don't discount it.

"The final target, or at least the final one we know of, is target five. He is the cook, whose job is outlined in the briefing notes. We expect him to remain at the olivar this morning. The arrest team need to be aware that this property is likely to have a large quantity of volatile and highly flammable liquids. He is a Barry Marshall, aged thirty-nine and a British citizen. He has minor drug convictions and it is not believed that he uses firearms.

"All targets must be arrested and taken to the five police stations as shown in the briefing notes in separate vehicles. I want them kept incommunicado and strip searches are to be conducted after initial body searches at the scenes.

"We are prepared to allow the team to move the containers to the warehouse. If the main suspects are at the warehouse after the arrival of the first container, then I will give the green light. No-one should do anything without my direct order to go. Is that clear?

"The tactical team will go to Biniaraix and wait at the designated area and should also go on my command, simultaneously with the Palma operation. There will be three scenes and each scene must be secured after the prisoners have been removed. The Scenes of Crime Units have been designated a crime scene each and under no circumstance do I want any team going to any other crime scene than the one they have been designated. I do not want any of these guys getting off due to cross-contamination of evidence. The armed tactical support units, except those designated as arresting officers, will remain at the scenes until stood down by me.

"I want all teams in place by eight o'clock. It is now ten past seven. I want to see inspectors only after this briefing. Are there any questions? No, then it just remains for me to say good luck, be safe and watch your backs out there."

Ramon gave a further short briefing to the team leaders, making sure they all understood their roles, and then all officers, including Ramon, made their way to their designated positions and waited.

It wasn't long before the first transmission was made.

"Oscar Charlie from Sierra Tango Two."

"Go ahead, Sierra Tango Two," said Ramon in Spanish.

"Just to confirm that the vessel you can see docking is *APL Columbia*."

"Vale, vale. Muy bien."

A short time later, the surveillance team at Marivent covering McClean, made contact.

"Oscar Charlie from Sierra Tango Three."

"Send, Sierra Tango Three."

"Target two has just left his apartment and has got into his black Porsche Cayenne and is driving east towards the port area. We are following."

"Received. All Sierra Tango and Alpha Tango units at the warehouse and dock area, be aware that target two is on his way to you now in his black Porsche Cayenne," said Ramon.

"Vale. Claro que sí."

Target two arrived and parked his vehicle at the docks close to the container ship and got out. Ramon was watching him from his vantage point at the Port Authority offices on the third floor of their building, from where he could see both the area where the containers were being unloaded and, with the use of binoculars and covert CCTV cameras, which had been set up especially for the operation, the areas inside and outside of the warehouse. He watched as McClean spoke to someone from the Port Authority who he appeared to show paperwork regarding the three containers. Ramon could then see McClean use his mobile phone and he returned and sat in his vehicle.

A few minutes later there was another radio transmission.

"Oscar Charlie from Sierra Tango One Alpha,"

"Go ahead," said Ramon.

"Targets one, three and four have just got into their black BMW X6 and are leaving the olivar. I am following with Bravo. Charlie and Delta call signs will remain with target five and their tactical support unit. Our tactical support unit is going to following us. We will keep you updated," said Juan.

"Okay. Keep your distance Sierra Tango One Alpha. I don't want them spooked," said Ramon.

"Por supuesto. Vale, vale jefe," replied Juan.

About half an hour later, Juan sent another transmission,

"Oscar Charlie from Sierra Tango One Alpha."

"Go ahead."

"Target vehicle has pulled into a side street off Carrer d'Alfons el Magnanim in Palma. Stand by. All three targets have left the vehicle and gone into a café on the main road, café Sa Cantina y Tu. They are now having some food at a table outside, over."

"All received, over and out." said Ramon.

"Oscar Charlie from Sierra Tango Three, target two has got out of his vehicle and is talking to the driver of a white Scania lorry. Target two has now got into the cab of the lorry, which is now driving towards the containers."

"Yes, I can see the vehicle," said Ramon.

"Oscar Charlie, both the lorry driver and target two are out of the vehicle and talking to a member of the port staff. A container is now being loaded onto the Scania lorry. Stand by. Both the target and the driver have returned to the cab of the vehicle and it is on the move. I am following the vehicle. It has crossed the flyover and is now travelling towards the warehouse. Units covering the warehouse, be advised that target two is in the cab of a white Scania lorry, vehicle registration mark 6952 HPV and will arrive at the warehouse compound within two minutes. Stand by. Scania lorry has just entered the warehouse compound. Target two has just opened the doors to the warehouse and the lorry is now backing up and has reversed inside. Target two has now closed the doors to the warehouse, over."

"From the covert cameras, I can see the container being unloaded. Can you get me details of the company which owns that Scania lorry, Control?" asked Ramon.

"Wilco, Comisario."

"Standby, the lorry is driving out of the warehouse. The driver is remaining in the cab but target two is now reclosing the doors. Target two is breaking the seal and opening the container. He appears to be checking the contents. Wait out. He is now on his mobile phone," said Ramon.

"Oscar Charlie from Sierra Tango One Alpha, target one has just received a phone call and all three targets are on the move, over."

"All received, Sierra Tango One Alpha. All units be advised targets are on the move," said Ramon. "Target two has left the warehouse and has returned to the cab of the lorry. Stand by Sierra Tango Three."

"Roger, Oscar Charlie. Vehicle looks as if it is going back for a second container. Wait. Suspect lorry has re-entered unloading area at port. Second container has been loaded onto lorry. Vehicle is now on the move. Heading back towards warehouse, over."

"Oscar Charlie from Sierra Tango One Alpha, target vehicle is now on Paseo Marítimo heading past the turn off for the docks. It looks as if it is heading to the warehouse. ETA is two minutes, over."

"Vale, vale.¡ Venga, va vamos! All units stand by, stand by," said Ramon. His heartbeat was getting faster. He could feel the adrenaline rushing through his body. *This was it; it was getting close*, he thought.

"Sierra Tango One Charlie, Delta and Alpha Tango India, be advised that when you hear my order for our units here in Palma, that is your order to enter the target premises in Biniaraix, claro?"

"Vale, claro que sí, Comisario."

"Sí, claro."

"Target vehicle now entering the compound to the warehouse. Vehicle now stopped and three targets have got out, from Sierra Tango One Alpha. All three have gone inside."

A few moments passed before Sierra Tango One Alpha continued,

"Scania lorry on the move with the second container. Stand by. Vehicle heading back to warehouse. Vehicle now approaching doors to warehouse with target two still in the cab. The doors have been closed, over."

"From Oscar Charlie, from the CCTV I can see target two out of the cab. He is talking to targets one and four. They have gone out of sight of the camera. Shit! Okay, they are walking back into shot. The second container has been taken off the back. The driver is still in his cab."

"Oscar Charlie from Control."

"Send, Control," said Ramon.

"The Scania lorry is registered to A&G Transporte, which is a vehicle and driver hire company from Son Bugadelles, over."

"Received. All units stand by. I can't see the targets. They are out of sight of the surveillance camera again. Shit!" said Ramon, getting anxious.

"From Sierra Tango One Alpha, the warehouse doors are opening and the lorry is leaving the compound. I can only see the driver in the cab, over."

"I need you to stop that vehicle at the docks, Sierra Tango One Alpha and arrest the driver. In the meantime, they are closing the doors to the warehouse. Okay, all units: Go! Go! Go!" shouted Ramon.

Ramon watched the unfolding scene nervously on his monitors. He could see several of the targets walk into the second container and out of his view. He could then see around ten police officers move to all sides of the warehouse. He could see a lead officer from the armed tactical support unit try the warehouse main doors, which appeared to be unlocked. He then saw him give a signal to his accompanying officers and about six entered the warehouse. He saw a flash on the monitor, as first a flash grenade and then a smoke grenade was thrown into the warehouse.

"Contact! Contact! Shots fired!" shouted a tactical support officer.

Ramon could hear the sound of automatic weapons being fired during the transmission. The smoke was now clouding the images from the CCTV system set up inside the warehouse. The covert microphones which had been installed had failed to pick up any earlier conversation clearly but it was now picking up the sound of automatic gunfire.

"I need a 'sitrep'! What's happening?" he shouted into his radio.

The gunfire continued unabated for several moments.

"Target down!" called an officer.

The gunfire stopped as quickly as it had started and Ramon could see his tactical support officers moving in towards the remaining targets. He could hear them shouting at the targets to get down on the ground and as the smoke started to clear, he could see two handcuffed targets in the prone position with armed officers standing over them.

"Oscar Charlie from Alpha Tango India,"

"Go ahead, over."

"Target five is under arrest and the premises are secure, over."

"Received," said Ramon. "Units in the warehouse, sitrep over," demanded Ramon.

"Oscar Charlie from Alpha Tango Sierra, we have two targets under arrest and another target has been shot and is critical. We need an ambulance to the scene, over."

"Only three targets? Which ones and where is the other target?"

"Target two, McClean and target three, Finn are under arrest. Target four, Knox has been shot. There is no sign of target one, Mason. We have secured the building. He must have been in the cab of the lorry, over."

"Sierra Tango One Alpha, are you hearing this? Target one must be in the lorry cab. What's happening?"

asked Ramon, looking at the monitor, which showed the lorry driving into the docks area with an unmarked police car following.

"Stand by, stand by," said Juan.

Ramon watched as Mason got out of the lorry. He could see him reach into his jacket and produce a weapon, which he thought appeared to look like an Uzi submachine-gun. He watched as the police vehicle came under fire. Both officers within it did not exit the vehicle. The tactical support vehicle behind it also then came under sustained automatic fire. He watched as Mason emptied his magazine, dropped his empty clip and reloaded with a fresh one and continued to fire at the second police vehicle.

"All units be advised, police need urgent assistance at the container area of Palma docks. Any unit not holding a scene or with a prisoner, make their way to this location immediately. Be advised, target one is in possession of an Uzi-type submachine-gun and is pinning officers down. Control, I need that ambulance diverted to that location and get another one for the injured target, over," said Ramon quickly.

"Wilco, Comisario."

Ramon continued to watch on his monitor. No officers exited the two vehicles and he could see Mason start running towards the quayside and then out of view of the CCTV system.

"Sierra Tango One Alpha or Bravo. Any unit at the docks, how many casualties have you got? What's happening?" asked Ramon in an exasperated tone.

"Medical assistance required boss. I am hit in the neck. Bravo has been hit twice in the leg. The tactical support vehicle doesn't look in great shape," said Juan, slowly.

"Oscar Charlie, this is Alpha Tango Sierra. Urgent medical assistance required. I am okay, as is my driver but he is working on Alpha Tango Delta, who has sustained a serious gunshot wound to the head, over."

"Shit! Received. Control, where's that ambulance? You may get at least two more to that scene asap," said Ramon. "All units be advised that target one has made off in the direction of the containers area of the dock-yard. Call signs from tactical support sniper unit, could you not get a clean shot?"

"Oscar Charlie from Alpha Tango Charlie, negative on that. The lorry cab blocked my whole view to the target. I had him in my sights momentarily but not long enough to take a shot from about four hundred metres away from the initial contact area. He then disappeared into warehouse G by the unloading area, over."

"All units, I need you to make your way to warehouse G at the docks. I need a cordon set up and I need 'Operation Lockdown' put in place. Control, I need you to instigate that and get me as many resources as you can. I need the police helicopter up and I think we need to circulate photographs of Mason to the media. He is too dangerous to be allowed to leave this area if he hasn't already done so. I also want a tracker dog down to this scene at the double. Clear?"

"¡Inmediatemente, Comisario!" replied the officer from the Control Room at Police Headquarters.

"I am leaving my position Control and going to assist the wounded officers," said Ramon, grabbing his police radio and making his way down the stairs to the scene of the shootings.

"Vale, Comisario."

Ramon ran the few hundred metres to a scene of devastation. Both unmarked police vehicles were riddled with bullet holes. One officer was desperately involved in CPR on a colleague who had been lifted from the car and was now lying on his back. His head and face were covered in blood. Ramon could see the entry wound in his forehead and he knew any attempt at reviving him was going to be fruitless. Just then, two ambulances with sirens blaring and lights flashing, pulled alongside the injured officers. Other police officers arrived in vehicles and on foot and approached Ramon for further instructions.

"Get down there! Warehouse G!" he bellowed, extremely annoyed at the outcome of the operation, no matter what the drugs haul would be. He quickly shouted after the officers who he had just berated, "Please, for God's sake be careful. Contain him if you find him and wait for back up. Okay, venga!" he said, ushering them onwards again.

Ramon turned around and watched as two paramedics continued to work on the officer with the gunshot wound to his head until they stopped and one looked up and shook his head. Ramon cursed into himself and turned to the officer's sergeant.

"He is the first man I have lost under my command. What was his name?" asked Ramon.

"Guillem Bernat. He had only been with this unit for six months. He had transferred in from Traffico because he was bored there."

"Has he a family?" asked Ramon, shaking his head in disgust.

"Yes, Comisario. He was married with two young children. They live in Santa Maria del Cami," replied the officer.

"Fuck! Leave it to me, Sergeant. I will inform them personally."

"Sir, I will do it, if you don't mind. I know his wife Maria well and I think it would be better coming from me."

"Very well, Sergeant. Thankyou. We will get this bastard if it is the last thing I do. I will personally see to that. Will you go with the body and sort out all the necessary paperwork?"

"Of course, sir."

Over the course of the next few hours, Ramon returned some order to the chaos of the scene that was apparent when he had initially arrived. During that time all wounded officers were taken to hospital and were now in a stable condition. He had been told that Knox had died of his injuries on his way to hospital. He had been in contact by phone with his equivalent in the National Crime Agency to appraise him of how the operation had panned out, only for him then to be told that Knox had been recruited by him as a paid informant but that contact had been lost between them two days previously. Ramon was furious at having been kept in the dark but he felt that knowing that would not have saved either Knox or his own officer.

A tracking police dog was brought to the scene but it failed to pick up any scent relating to Mason. An operation was now well under way, consisting of around fifty armed officers going from house to house and building to building, working their way towards Warehouse G, systematically searching all possible places where the target could be hiding. Initial enquiries at the warehouse had shown that Mason had entered the building and was then seen leaving by a rear fire door. Police throughout the whole city and the island were on high alert. News bulletins on local television had shown a picture of Mason, telling the public to be on the lookout for him but not to approach him.

The contents of the three containers had been taken to a police property warehouse and initial reports of a sample checked at the scene was that it was indeed cocaine and intelligence estimates were proving to be accurate on the quantity seized. The three targets arrested were now in police custody at stations in the city, as well as the driver of the lorry.

Ramon had not eaten since five o'clock that morning and that was now twelve hours ago. He didn't feel like eating. He felt sick to his stomach that a young officer had lost his life to a criminal who had not given him a chance in order to avoid capture for him breaking the law, and all for what? For financial gain? He was at a loss at how some people did not seem to realise how precious human life was and that they were prepared to take the lives of anyone who stood between them and what they wanted. He couldn't enjoy a meal until this animal was caught but he realised that he needed to eat something if he was going to do his job properly.

With all scenes being held until he released his officers, he returned to his office at Police Headquarters to organise the interview schedule for the prisoners in custody. He managed to get some sustenance from a meal at the police canteen and then he made a dreaded phone call to his boss, el Director Adjunto Operativo, explaining the outcome of the operation. His superior passed on his condolences for the loss of the officer in the line of duty but congratulated him nevertheless on the volume of the drug haul. He tried to console Ramon by saying that he was sure that he had done everything in his power to protect his officers but that automatically there had to be an internal investigation into the murder of the officer and the shooting of Knox. All police resources were promised to assist in the capture of Mason and then Ramon was left to his own thoughts back at his desk. The time was now nearly eight o'clock. He started to set out an interview schedule for the prisoners in custody when his mobile phone rang. It was James Gordon from Fornalutx. Ramon was going to let it go to voicemail and then he remembered how James had almost been killed by criminals just like Mason and he quickly had a change of heart and chided himself for even contemplating such a thing and answered.

"Hey, James. How are you?" he asked glumly.

"Hey, Ramon. I am sorry to bother you. I know you must be extremely busy and I won't keep you long but I am in Palma, driving towards my houseboat which has just run out of Butano gas and I couldn't stop myself from ringing. How did this morning go?" asked James, enthusiastically.

"Not great, James. We got a huge quantity of cocaine. We arrested most of the targets but the main player is on the run. Knox is dead and the annoying thing is, he was working with the NCA after all and they lied to me. There was a shoot-out and I lost an officer today. Several others are still in hospital but they are thankfully out of danger. I am just feeling down because is a haul of drugs worth the life of a good officer? For me, no," said Ramon.

"Oh, Ramon, I am sorry to hear that but you owe it to that officer's family to secure convictions of these criminals, but you are right, his life was not worth the haul. Remember, you didn't pull the trigger and we all knew the risks when we joined our respective police services. I know that is cold comfort but without people like you and your officers who put their lives on the line, often without much thanks from the public, there would be chaos and lawlessness. Anyway, who is the main player that is on the run?" asked James.

"I thought I told you about him, no? Look, I will send you his details and his photograph to your phone. Have you not seen all the news bulletins on television today?" asked Ramon.

"Sorry Ramon, I tend not to watch Spanish TV," said James sheepishly.

James could hear Ramon talking away from the phone before he said,

"Sorry James, I have to go. A report has just come in of an armed car-jacking in Marivent and police are giving chase. I think it is our man. Adiós."

The line went dead before James could say good luck but he appreciated Ramon's task was urgent. He drove along the Paseo Marítimo and noticed that there were uniformed police officers at almost every junction. He continued and he could hear the sound of sirens ahead in the distance as he stopped at a set of red traffic lights in the outside lane of the three lanes, city bound. The sirens were getting closer and ahead he could see the blue flashing lights of a police car. He watched as a dark-coloured vehicle travelling at high speed was weaving in and out of traffic on the opposite carriageways heading in his direction. He then saw the dark-coloured vehicle clip another vehicle and then it appeared to lose control and was heading directly for him in his stationary position. At that point everything went into slow motion and he could see the headlights of the car directly in front of him as the car inexorably hurtled towards him at speed.

Chapter 13

The Party

The front door opened and James walked in. The small terraced house was crammed with party-goers and James made his way to the kitchen and grabbed a bottle of beer and opened it. A strange feeling came over him all of a sudden and he realised he was standing in the kitchen of a house that he did not recognise. He felt very peculiar. There was loud music emanating from upstairs with a base so deep that it was causing the bottles of beer on the kitchen worktop to vibrate. He looked around him. There were several other people in the kitchen chatting and a couple of the women were looking over at him and smiling. He could see their lips moving, as they were in conversation but he couldn't hear them talking and it wasn't just down to the loudness of the music. Just then, a man in his early thirties approached him. He was smiling at James and appeared to know him, as his body language was that of someone familiar with him. He was talking to James but he had just the sound of ringing in his ears.

He had never seen the man before, who patted James on the shoulder and laughed as if he had just told a joke. James walked off from the man and opened the kitchen door. The house was thick with cigarette smoke and the strong, putrid smell of cannabis. He walked into another room on the ground floor, where several men were sitting watching a porn film, while a couple were kissing passionately on a sofa, unencumbered. One man looked around at him and beckoned him to join them. James looked vacantly at the man before he turned around and walked back into the small hall of the house.

He stared up the staircase and slowly began to walk up the stairs. He noted that the wallpaper was peeling off in several places, revealing black mould underneath and the carpet on the stairs was excessively dirty and threadbare. Discarded cigarette butts were strewn all over the stairs and landing in a quantity that he had never seen before. He squeezed past several people on the stairs; most of whom glanced towards him and smiled. One pretty girl, in her late twenties he guessed, was pointing up the stairs and saying something inaudible to him.

He continued and walked along the first-floor landing which had four doors, two on each side of the landing. All the doors were closed. He opened the first door and his ears were at once subjected to the throb of the loud base music. He had discovered its source. Several men were standing behind a mixing deck and were playing vinyl records on two turntables while passing a joint among one another. When James entered, one man with a large scar on his face smiled while pointing and shooting imaginary pistols. James turned, walked out and closed the door behind him but his clarity of hearing still didn't return. The thumping beat in his head remained, just slightly less intense.

James crossed the narrow hallway and opened the second door. It was a bedroom with a double bed, with only a small, low watt bedside lamp casting meagre light onto proceedings. A young black man was having sex with an older white woman. Neither stopped, nor seemed put out by their voyeuristic intruder. The woman, who was on top, looked around at James and smiled and beckoned him towards her. He turned around and walked out, closing the door behind him. He walked the few feet to the next door and pushed down on the handle. It was locked. He started walking towards the last door, when from behind him, he heard the lock being unbolted and he turned around to see a woman in her late twenties, standing in the doorway and smiling at him. She walked towards him and grabbed him by the hand and both entered the room.

It was another dimly lit bedroom and the woman closed the door behind them and locked it with a bolt. She was a pretty girl, albeit she looked older than her years. She was wearing a black camisole top and knickers and was looking directly into his eyes. She pushed him onto the bed and reached into the inside pocket of his jacket and produced a brown zip up pouch. She then proceeded to empty the contents of a small cling film wrap onto the bedside table and started making two lines with white powder using a credit card. She produced a £10 note from the bedside cabinet drawer, rolled it up and snorted a line of cocaine up her nose, wiping the end of her nose after doing so. She then smiled and reached the rolled up note to James. He paused but then found himself leaning over the white powder and he snorted the remaining line of cocaine.

What am I doing? he thought.

The girl pushed him onto his back on the bed and straddled him. She then took off her camisole top and started kissing him. Before long, she was helping him off with his clothes and a short time later they were engaged in sexual intercourse. James did not seem able to stop what was going on. He was not getting any enjoyment from this act. He had no idea who the woman was or what he was doing there. He had an over-riding feeling of guilt and remorse when it was over. He stood up and got dressed, as the woman lit a cigarette and reached over and took a drink from his half-empty beer bottle on the bedside table. He lifted the brown zip up pouch and replaced it in the inside pocket of his jacket, walked to the door, unlocked the bolt and walked out, without turning round to the girl.

He closed the door behind him and walked slowly back along the landing and back down the stairs. What had just happened? He had just had unprotected sex with a woman he didn't recognise, and taken cocaine. He had seen cocaine numerous times in his former career in the drug squad but throughout his service he had not actually seen users take it, never mind take it himself. The closest he had come to experiencing what he had just done was when he had watched it in films. His head felt very strange and James didn't think it was solely down to having taken cocaine for the first time.

He walked back into the kitchen and lifted another bottle of beer from the kitchen worktop and opened it. He took several long mouthfuls, in an effort to wash out the fuzziness from his head. Moments later, the woman with whom he had just had sex with walked in, fully clothed and approached him giving him a long and lasting kiss, before grabbing a bottle of beer for herself and then she left the kitchen. James then heard a deafening bang, as if the front door had just been forced off its hinges followed by a loud thud against the solid outside kitchen door. He opened a door to a walk-in cupboard and held it shut from inside. From his position in the confined space in the dark he could hear screams and the sound of people running from the property, to the front and to the rear of the house. After a short while there was only silence to keep him company. The silence was occasionally peppered with a scream or shout but they seemed like a long way away from him.

He opened the cupboard door and walked into the deserted kitchen. The door to the rear yard had been forced open. He peered into the dark yard. There was no-one or nothing visible. He walked tentatively into the yard. The rear gate was open and he peered into the pitch-black alley. He could see the dim, soft orange glow of a street light at the end of the alley to one end and walked slowly towards the light. At the end of the alley, he peered around the corner in both directions. There was no-one in sight. He crossed the street to the other side where the small terraced houses had even smaller front gardens with low wooden fences. He could hear voices getting closer, so he quickly stepped over a low fence and knelt down in the garden. He removed his brown zip up pouch and threw it into bushes of the adjoining garden and lay flat on his stomach, peering between the gaps in the wooden picket fence. James' heart was now racing. Why had he just thrown away a pouch? He was feeling incredibly guilty. He just wanted to go home. He could hear voices and the barks of dogs getting closer to him fast. He closed his eyes and wished he was somewhere else.

The sound of dogs barking right above his head made him open his eyes. He was immediately blinded by a strong white light being shone into his eyes. He realised that police officers were standing above him and straight away he was being pinned to the ground and a pair of handcuffs were then placed tightly on his wrists behind his back. He was unceremoniously lifted to his feet by two officers and he noted that other officers were shining torches into the neighbouring garden. One officer then held up the brown zip up pouch that he had discarded moments earlier. James was then marched roughly towards a police van and pushed inside, causing him to fall on his front. He heard the door being locked behind him and soon he felt the van move off.

A short time later, the van came to a stop and he heard the rear doors open and once again James was lifted to his feet and taken into a custody suite of an unfamiliar police station. Some clarity of hearing was being restored to him but his vision was still blurred. He assumed that this was due to his alcohol and drug consumption. He was booked in and a custody record was opened for him.

"What is your full name, as if I didn't know?" asked the custody sergeant, in a strong Geordie accent.

"My name is James Gordon. I live in Mallorca and I am a former police officer. I have no idea how I got here, or why I was at that house. Can you tell me where I am please?" asked James.

"That's a good one, isn't it 'Smurf'?" replied the custody sergeant, laughing with the arresting officer.

"You are in Hotel Shit and this is Shagaluf," he continued, drawing more laughter from his colleagues. "Right Mason, I need you to listen to what this officer has to say. Right Smurf, fire away."

"Serg, as a result of information received, we attended number ten Hillingdon Street on the Pennywell Estate with a warrant under the Misuse of Drugs Act, 1971. On entry, a large number of people fled the premises and officers gave chase. The prisoner was seen exiting the rear of the premises and was observed crossing the street and then seen to throw a brown pouch into the garden of number twenty-three, before lying down in the garden of number twenty-one, which is where he was found and detained. A search of the area of the bushes in number twenty-three was conducted and this pouch, item of evidence PD1 was recovered. It is described as a brown zip up pouch with forty-five small clear plastic wraps containing white powder. It is my belief that the white powder is cocaine. He was arrested and cautioned at ten past ten and he replied, 'You can fuck right off you twat'."

"You have heard what this officer has had to say. Is there anything you want to say in reply to this allegation?" asked the custody officer, in a matter-of-fact way.

"Yes, I do. Firstly, I have not been arrested or cautioned, and secondly, I need to speak to the duty inspector. I don't know who you think I am but my name is James Gordon..." started James, before being interrupted.

"Very good and I'm Santa Claus. Here is a notice explaining your rights,"

"Stop being such an asshole!" shouted James. "Get me the duty inspector now!"

James was beginning to get very angry. He had no idea why he was in a custody suite, obviously somewhere in the north-east of England, judging by the accents of the officers. Their joviality at his expense was beginning to wear thin.

"If you even think about searching me or authorising an intimate search on me, you have another thing coming, until I speak to a solicitor and the duty inspector," said James, trying very hard to regain some semblance of calm.

His arms were then grabbed by an officer on each side of him. James tensed his muscles and tried to struggle free. One of the officers was putting great force on the handcuffs still around his wrists, behind his back. He could feel them cutting into his wrists, which made him angrier still and then his head was forced forward onto the counter of the custody suite and his arms were forced upwards, causing him significant pain.

"Aaaghh! You bastards! Let me out of these cuffs and we'll see what big men you are then!" he shouted, as he tried not to show signs of weakness but the pain was excruciating.

Another officer joined the melee and started searching him with his hands in a pair of disposable rubber gloves and he was removing all items from James' pockets and setting them on the counter beside his head. James heard the door to the custody suite open and another voice behind him said,

"Ah come on Tony man, we don't need all this hassle tonight. Easy lads, easy. Look, if I get these guys to release their grip, do you promise to behave yourself? Come on Tony, you've been caught banged to rights

man and I want to get home this evening as long as the doctor says you're fit for interview."

James stopped tensing his muscles and slowly the officers released their grip on his arms and head. He turned to his right and there was a man in a brown leather jacket with stubble and grey hair, smiling at him.

"Come on Tony. I've always be fair to you, so you be fair to me. You know who I am don't you?"

James shook his head.

"Away man. I'm DS Billy McWhirter of the drug squad as well you know. What bloody hallucinogenic crap have you been takin' tonight? I've not seen you this bad before. Listen Joe, I'd rather he was seen by the doctor as soon as possible, to see if he deems him fit for interview. Any attempt at an intimate search is only going to set him off again. I will keep an eye on him until the doc sees him and he can keep his cuffs on, if you wish."

"Okay Billy but I need you to sign the custody record to that effect."

"No problem. Is the doc around?"

"He's just in with another one. He won't be long." Turning to James he said, "I've listed all the property taken from your possession. Have a read and tell me if you're happy with that."

"Fine," replied James, moving his neck from side to side.

A door opened and another prisoner left the doctor's room.

"Right, the doctor will see you now," said the custody sergeant.

After being deemed fit for interview, James was shown into an interview room, where DS McWhirter and a female officer where already inside.

"Take a seat Tony," he said.

James sat down at the interview table. DS McWhirter came around behind him with a set of handcuff keys in his hand.

"I am prepared to take these off you but at the first sign of trouble they go straight back on and you get banged up till morning. Okay, Tony?"

"Fair enough."

The handcuffs were removed and James brought his arms round to his front and he rubbed his reddened and cut wrists and was about to give off about his treatment and then he thought, *what's the point?*

"Can I just confirm you have elected to proceed with this interview without the presence of a solicitor?" asked the female detective.

"That's correct."

Having had time to consider his options, James had just wanted to get things over with as quickly as possible and had told DS McWhirter his change of plan whilst waiting for the doctor to see him. The interview was mostly a blur for James. He was answering all questions but it was clear his answers were being met with derision by both detectives. He did not believe what was happening. They kept calling him 'Tony'. Once the interview was over and the tape machine was switched off, James turned to DS McWhirter and said,

"Humour me here. What is my full name?" asked James.

"Really? Okay. Tony Mason."

"Where do I live?"

"You have several houses but you spend most of your time around various addresses on the Pennywell Estate in Sunderland."

"This is unbelievable! Okay, I can prove it to you. Get me a mirror, please," said James.

The female Detective looked at her boss and he nodded. She reached into her handbag and took out her make-up compact, opened it and handed it to James. He held it up to his face and froze, for staring back at him was the face of a stranger.

Chapter 14

Light at the End of the Tunnel

What is that awful music? thought James. *It is going over and over again.*

He was beginning to get annoyed by the repetition of the familiar sound of songs that he recognised as ones he had on a playlist on his iPod. This was one cause for disgruntlement but when added to muscular discomfort and a beeping noise constantly in his head, it was becoming almost untenable. He opened his eyes and looked around him. He felt rather odd. His vision was slightly blurred and the room appeared out of focus. This was nothing new to a man who was short-sighted and who only wore his prescription glasses when it was absolutely essential. In fact, his glasses and sunglasses spent more time on his head than over his eyes. Contact lenses for him were another source of frustration and were only worn once a week during his weekly game of football. He normally spent the whole game with impaired vision, as either one would fall out after heading a ball, or he would insert them back to front or, equally frustratingly, put them in the wrong eye as each lens had a slightly different prescription strength. This was slightly different and more severe. Normally, only the edges of things in the distance would be blurred. His whole vista, near and far was quite simply fuzzy.

His mouth was dry and he tried to move his arms up to his mouth but they didn't quite make it for some reason.

James cleared his throat, which was feeling sore and irritated, and suddenly he could see the outline of a figure, which had previously been just a dark shape in the middle distance, move towards him. He then heard a voice he recognised as that of Charlotte say,

"He's awake. Oh my God, James you're awake!"

James' brain struggled to compute her words. He wondered if he'd had a very long lie-in and had just woken up and was going to be met with words of chastisement from Charlotte. What came next took him by surprise. She approached him at his bedside and took his hand tenderly. He could see her face more clearly now and he looked up to apologise for such a long sleep but there was no sign of admonishment in her face but rather she was crying and wiping her tears with her other hand. Her crying became harder, which concerned him greatly.

"What's wrong Charlotte? What's wrong?" he attempted to say but his words seemed to be slurred and he didn't recognise his own voice.

His nose felt sore and he managed to slowly touch it with his left hand. He felt a tube going in through his nose. Slowly the penny began to drop.

"Am I in hospital?" he murmured.

"Yes, James you...give me a minute."

She turned away and James could see her head shaking slightly. James gripped her hand slightly harder and she turned back to him.

"I thought we had lost you," she said, forcing her words out. "I want to kiss you but I'm scared I might disrupt some of your tubes. Listen, I need to go and get a doctor. Wait a minute, I can use the 'Call' button. Charlotte frantically pressed a button near the bed. "I have to get someone and I need to get the boys in here. Don't you go back to sleep. Stay awake. I will be back in one minute," she said smiling between crying and kissing his hand.

James could hear Charlotte outside his room, calling for help. He then heard her calling for his sons, Adam and Reuben. He kept his head looking in the same direction to his side but slowly moved it round and stared to the front. Before he could see who was there, he was aware there was a plethora of people around him and he realised that the annoying constant beeping in his head was a heart monitor. He soon realised that he also had a feeding tube up his nose. It was hooked up to a ventilator and a tube was down his windpipe through his mouth, and he had a drip attached to his arm. Some clarity of vision was beginning to return and he could see several doctors or nurses checking his monitors and they were asking him how he felt.

"I'm pretty sore all over," he replied. "My throat is sore and very dry. Can I have a drink and could I have this tube removed from my throat by any chance?"

"Yes, I can do that for you," said the doctor, putting on surgical gloves. After some discomfort the breathing tube was removed and a nurse by his bedside electronically raised the top half of his bed.

"That's better. That's what was making it hard to talk clearly."

The nurse put a glass of water in front of him and placed the straw in his mouth and he took several small sips.

"Gracias," he said.

"De nada," she replied smiling.

Just then, the door swung open gently and Charlotte returned along with James' two boys, who he could see had very red eyes and were struggling to keep their emotions in check. He thought they had obviously been asked to stay back while the medical staff checked his condition, but he couldn't contain his delight at seeing them.

"Hello boys! That must have been a pretty strong curry I had but I'm okay now," he said, smiling at the boys.

Adam wiped his eyes and said, "Glad you're going to be okay, Dad. We love you, you know?" before he spluttered and fell into a bout of seemingly uncontrollable sobbing, which then set Reuben off in a similar manner, while Charlotte tried to console both boys, hugging them and saying,

"Dad is going to be fine. His brain just told him that he needed a long sleep."

James looked at Reuben and Adam and said, "These good people will be finished shortly I'm sure. Won't you?" he enquired hopefully.

"Very soon, Señor Gordon. We just need to monitor your breathing, your body temperature and your heart beat among other things. Have you any specific pain anywhere in your body? I am Doctor Rodriguez but you can call me Jésus."

"By all accounts, it sounds as if I was very nearly talking to another Jésus," said James, attempting a smile. "Anyway my ribs and abdomen are quite sore, and my neck."

"They almost certainly would be when someone is in a collision with a fast moving vehicle head on, when their car is stationary and their car is then crumpled when it is pushed backwards into a stationary lorry. To make things worse, it is my understanding that you were then hit with the force of the other driver coming through your windshield. You had two Butano gas bottles in the boot of your car. The severity of the impact caused one of them to explode but the driver of the other car took the full impact of that explosion and ultimately that saved your life. You are a very fortunate man, Señor Gordon. God has been watching over you. You have been in a coma for seventeen days. The brain does, as your wife says, shut down the body functions, as a way of self-preservation. Some comas are very short. Some unfortunate people never come out of them.

"I think it would be remiss of me not to tell you that when the ambulance crew arrived at the scene, technically you were dead for about a minute. You went into cardiac arrest and after CPR didn't work, a defibrillator had to be used several times to let's call it, jump start your heart. You were flat-lining. I have increased the pain relief drug that we are giving you intravenously. It may make you slightly drowsy shortly. The pain in your abdomen is from the seatbelt and the steering wheel, even though the airbags inflated. Your neck and spine have whiplash injuries but these should not be long-lasting but you will need to come back on a regular basis to check the alignment of your spine, once the swelling has reduced. Your neck brace must remain on until your muscles, tendons and ligaments have healed significantly. Then you will need physiotherapy and massages. I have to say, all-in-all, you have come out of this remarkably unscathed. It may not feel like that now but trust me it could have been a lot worse. I will leave you now in peace and I'll check back with you later. Welcome back James," said the doctor with a smile, before leaving with the two nurses.

"What a lovely man," said James. "Come here you lot," he said, as his family all gathered close to him, with each of his sons giving him a long hug, followed by Charlotte, who kissed him gently and lovingly on the lips.

"Do you remember anything about what happened?" she asked.

"I can't remember anything. From what the doctor said, I was in a road traffic collision but where?" asked James.

"You were taking two bottles of gas up to the house-boat in Palma and it happened on Paseo Marítimo. It appears you were stopped at a set of traffic lights just before the cathedral and police were chasing the drug suspect from their earlier operation; the one that shot and killed a young cop who was working with Ramon. He has been up to see you twice, you know. Anyway, witnesses and the pursuing police told Ramon that the guy's car hit another car and he lost control of his and ended up crashing into you, head on. He wasn't wearing a seat belt and he went through his windscreen, through your windscreen and more than likely hit you on impact. The driver of the lorry behind you saw it all. He told Ramon that the guy ended up half in the parcel shelf and half in the back seat of your car, and then there was an almighty explosion as one of the Butano bottles exploded, but the guy absorbed the whole impact. Needless to say, he was killed instantly, if the initial impact hadn't already killed him. Our car is a right-off."

"I don't remember any of this," said James, looking worried.

"It is not uncommon for people to lose their memory having gone through a traumatic experience like this. It will take time but things may start to come back to you. The police at the scene apparently were really good. We need to send them and the paramedics something to say thank you. I have got their details," said Charlotte, looking in her handbag.

"Yes we definitely should. So what happened then?" asked James frowning, as he could not understand being unable to recall any of what Charlotte was telling him.

"Apparently, with the impact you went into cardiac arrest. The police made the decision to pull you from the car after the first explosion and everything. The ambulance was on the scene within minutes and they were working on you for ages and, as the doctor said, they had to use a defibrillator to get your heart beating again. They said you were clinically dead for about a minute," said Charlotte, watching James closely. She was aware that what she was telling him was a lot for anyone to take in and she didn't want to overload him with details.

"Continue, please. I need to know what happened to me. It may help me remember and I want to remember. I need to remember," said James, getting exasperated.

"Only if you're sure," she said, reaching forward and holding his hand.

"Yes, please go on," he said, looking up at her.

"Well, that's about it, other than you were brought to the Clínica Juaneda hospital here in Palma and you have been in a coma until just now. Your sisters have all been out to see you, and my dad and lots of friends from the valley wanted to come but I posted a message on Facebook to ask them not to," she said, lifting her mobile phone and taking a picture of him.

"Really? You could have warned me," said James, smiling.

"I need to post a photo on Facebook and tell everyone the good news. It is much easier than phoning round everyone."

"Okay. Fair enough. Listen, you mentioned a guy that was killed. Who was he?" asked James.

"Perhaps we should talk about that later," said Charlotte, nodding towards the boys.

"Come here again guys. I had a sort of tunnel vision there. I actually didn't see you standing there. I still feel a bit groggy but come and see me," said James, grinning.

His sons pulled over chairs and sat by James' bedside.

"That must have been tough for you guys as well. I hope you didn't miss too much school," said James, taking a hand of each of his sons and holding it for a short while.

"We have been coming with mum, but after school. The doctors said they would ring us if you woke up," said Adam.

"I have something for you, Dad," said Reuben, reaching over to the bedside cabinet. He lifted a large card and handed it to James.

"Wow! That's amazing. 'Millora't aviat.' What does that mean Reuben?" he asked.

"Don't you know?" replied Reuben, laughing. "It means get well soon."

"That's a great drawing on the front. Look at all these names. Did all your classmates sign it?" James asked, looking inside.

Reuben nodded with pride.

"Isn't that lovely? You will be able to tell them that your dad said 'moltes gràcies' and is now well enough to sit up. Thank you Reuben," said James, giving his son's hand a gentle squeeze.

"I did something for you too, Dad," said Adam.

"That's great, Adam."

"I brought in your iPod and put it in its docking station and have been playing your favourite playlist over and over again. The doctor said sometimes people in a coma come round faster if they hear voices or music that they are familiar with. I talked to you sometimes as well but usually I just played you your songs."

"Adam, I am not just saying this but I actually heard those songs. I think it really did help me wake up. I couldn't tell you what songs you played but I remember I was getting irritated by them being played over and over again and then I woke up, so thank you for that. It really helped," said James sincerely.

"Really! I think I'm going to cry again," said Adam, feeling very chuffed with himself.

"Boys, I think your dad needs his rest. It's been a very eventful day but he will need to take things easy for a while. Adam, take this and go and get you and Reuben something to drink from the machine at the end of the hall and wait for me there. I'm not going to be long. I need to get you back so you can do your homework and have supper," said Charlotte.

"Bye Dad. See you tomorrow," said Adam, giving his dad a hug.

"Bye Dad. Glad that you didn't die," said Reuben, hugging him too, drawing a smile from James with his turn of phrase.

"I'm glad I didn't die too. See you both tomorrow."

Charlotte sat beside James and took his hand.

"You gave us one hell of a scare. I know you were just in the wrong place at the wrong time but this stuff with Ramon and you getting involved with criminals; it has to stop. Your sons need their father and I need you. I thought you were gone for sure or if you did wake up that you might be in a vegetative state. Please think about this, James. It is important. You are no longer a police officer. There was a policeman killed that day and other officers seriously wounded and Ramon told me that the guy who you ran into on your scooter was killed too. Jimmy Knox, I think he said his name was."

"Jimmy Knox," interrupted James. "I know that name. Yes, I remember, I found his wallet and then Ramon and I went to the airport and he had drugs. The plaster cast. The drug shipment. There was to be an operation, you know a drugs bust. Was that the same day as my accident?" he asked with anticipation.

"Yes, it was later that same day, early evening."

"I'm beginning to remember a few things."

"That's great James but listen, I don't want you just lying hear thinking about police work. Remember what I said please and get some rest," said Charlotte firmly.

"Rest! I've been asleep for seventeen days or whatever it was. I need to remember. There is something in my head that I am trying to remember but I can't and it's very annoying."

"Before I go, I'm going to get the nurse to check in with you. Is there anything you need or anything you want me to bring you from home?" asked Charlotte.

"Home? No, not that I can think of. Shit! The hotel. I completely forgot we had a hotel! Who's been looking after things while I've been doing a Rip van Winkle?" he said, getting flustered.

"Calm yourself. It's fine. Monica has been an angel. She is quite happy to cover to let me get away to see you, and her sister has been doing some hours too. Everything is fine. I will come and see you early evenings until you are ready to be discharged, unless there is something that you need during the day, in which case I can slip away. Don't worry. You need to be relaxing and getting your strength back. Which reminds me, are you hungry?" asked Charlotte.

"You know I wasn't particularly until you mentioned it but yes, I'm starving."

"You would think they could remove the saline drip. I will ask the nurse if they can do that. Okay, see you tomorrow," said Charlotte, leaning over to kiss him and giving him a lingering look.

"I know. See you tomorrow," he said looking up at her.

A few minutes later, the nurse returned with the doctor and it was agreed that James could have a small amount of solid food and he felt much more comfortable once he had had it. The saline drip would remain for another day or so, as would the intravenous drip for his pain relief but he would be assessed the following day. It was likely that he would need to stay in hospital for a week or so but he felt that this was a minor inconvenience considering what he had just been through.

He still felt weak and drifted off to sleep very quickly.

The following morning, he woke and looked at the wall clock opposite his bed. It was a quarter to eleven. He pressed the call button. A short time later a nurse came in.

"Good morning! Good morning! It is nice to see you awake. My name is Marianne. I have been looking after you with my other colleagues but it was my day off yesterday. It is a remarkable thing. Your wife is lovely and your sons: muchachos muy guapos! Just like their father I think, when he is better, eh?" said Marianne with a wink.

"Easy Marianne, you don't want to give me a heart attack, do you?" said James with a cheeky grin.

"So, tell me; what can I do for you?" she asked.

"I need to go to the toilet."

"Vale. Is it number ones or number twos?" she asked, counting with her fingers.

"Just a number one," said James, feeling a bit like a schoolboy.

"It's no problem. You can use this container. That's what it is for. When you need a number two, you can use a bedpan or you can get up and go to the toilet. We can help you with the drips. It's easy. ¿Todo bien?"

"Thanks."

"I will be back in two minutes with your breakfast. You had a good sleep last night. Normally we like patients to be awake early but you needed a good sleep, not like the sleep in a coma. See you soon," she said, giving James some privacy.

After enjoying his breakfast in bed, the doctor called in to check on James and it appeared he was making good progress.

"Doctor, can I have the drips removed today? They are quite restrictive. I hate needles or anything puncturing my skin," asked James.

"Not today, James. It is important that we can easily administer your pain relief but more importantly that we give you mannitol. You may have cerebral oedema, which is a swelling of the brain and it helps to reduce the pressure on your brain. We are also giving you dexamethasone, which is an anti-inflammatory steroid. You see James, you received quite a bang to the front of your skull and at best you have severe concussion. You do not have a fracture, which is good but head injuries can be potentially dangerous because there can be a slow leakage of blood from damaged blood vessels into or around the brain. This is what we refer to as subdural hematoma. There are other types of problems that can arise and these could require surgery, so it is important we continue to monitor your vital signs. I am happy with the progress you are making but I cannot do what you have asked today. I think it is important that patients understand why we do certain things," said Jésus.

"Thank you for explaining that for me. I understand. Your English is very good. I wish my Spanish was even half that good," said James, shaking his head gently.

"I did have the advantage of studying English at school in Madrid and then attending Nottingham University to read medicine."

"Really? I thought you were Mallorcan."

"My mother is from Barcelona and my father is from Madrid, which is where I grew up."

"It must be difficult in their house watching 'el clásico' you know, in football?" asked James.

"No! It is not a problem. My mother loves Barcelona and my father supports Athlético Madrid, so he supports Barcelona just in el clásico," he replied, laughing. "Anyway James, It is nice to talk with you. I am happy with your progress. There is nothing to worry about but we need to be cautious. Okay?"

"Okay. Oh Doctor, there is one thing. Can I have a mirror?" asked James.

"You want to look at your face? Your beard is coming on nicely. There isn't much visible swelling but sure, just a moment," he replied, leaving the room and returning with a hand-held mirror which he handed to James.

James held it up to his face and stared at his reflection. He had a few minor cuts to his face. He needed to use his beard trimmer to tackle his two and a half weeks of extra growth and he looked tired, despite having slept well the previous night. Despite not looking his best, he was relieved to see his familiar face. Just at that moment, he put the mirror down.

"I've just remembered why I wanted the mirror. It is coming back to me. I had a most horrible dream, not last night though. It must have been when I was in a coma. Oh Jésus, it was awful! It was so detailed and vivid and I was doing some terrible things and...that's right, I looked in a mirror and it wasn't my face. I can remember that face extremely well but I had never seen it before. I will never forget it now," said James energetically, feeling pleased that his short-term memory was coming back to him.

"This is a good sign; the fact that you are remembering things again. Would you like me to get you a pencil and paper? Maybe it would help you to try and draw the face. It is good to exercise your brain for parts of the day during your recovery but your brain also needs to rest at other times."

"Yes. I think I would like to try anyway," replied James.

"Give me a moment and I'll send one of the nurses in with that for you. See you later."

"Thanks Jésus."

A few minutes later, his nurse Marianne returned and handed him a pencil and a pad of paper. James raised his bed up and stared blankly at the page. He started to sketch a man's face and used the eraser on the end of his pencil as much as he drew but slowly the features of the man's face he had seen when he looked in the mirror were reappearing to him on the page. The more he drew, the more of his vivid dream was coming back to him. He started making notes of things that he remembered, as he drew on a page overleaf. Soon he was building up a picture with his words as well as his sketch. He started to have flashbacks and he recoiled with guilt when remembering his drug-taking and sexual encounter. He remembered the name that the police were calling him: Tony Mason, and he wrote it down.

After having his lunch, James continued. He thought it was good therapy and was helping his recovery. He finished his sketch and was quite impressed with his artistic skills. He touched up a couple of the features and shaded in a few more places but overall he was happy that it looked like 'his man'. He turned the page and realised he had amassed a considerable amount of words in list format. Amongst his words, some stood out to him: the Pennywell Estate in Sunderland, Hillingdon Street and DS Billy McWhirter.

James stared at these words on the page.

"Sunderland, Sunderland," he said to himself. *I was in Sunderland to chaperone Jimmy Knox on the plane when it all went tits up! That must be where all this has come from in my subconscious. I must have seen signs for the street and the estate when I was there*, he thought to himself. This made him feel relieved. He had answered the questions he had in his head and was satisfied with his conclusions and set the pad down on his bed.

He switched on the television on the wall opposite with the remote control and flicked through numerous Spanish channels until he came to a Spanish soap opera, as it was the best of a bad bunch. He became glued to it as the acting was very amateurish and every scene seemed to have twice the number of extras that was necessary but it amused him and passed the time before Charlotte and his sons were due to visit him in three hours.

Half an hour into the programme, his nurse, Marianne walked in.

"Hey, James. You have a visitor but I wanted to see if you want to see him. He is a friend, not family: Ramon Martinez."

"That's fine, Marianne. You can show him in," he said, turning down the volume.

"Knock, knock," said Ramon, putting his head around the door.

"Ramon! Come in. Nice to see you."

"I heard the great news and I hope you don't mind. I never know what to bring when visiting someone in hospital so I brought you some flowers, some fresh fruit and some chocolate," he said, setting the items down on

James' trolley at the end of the bed, before turning to the television behind him. "You are watching *María la del Barrio*? It is a dreadful telenovela," he said, sitting down. "You are looking much better than a few days ago when I saw you amigo."

"I am feeling better today than yesterday. The staff here are great, and I'm making good progress according to the doctor, so I have to be thankful because I know things could have turned out very differently."

"I know, my friend, I know. You are a lucky guy. I saw the state of your car and when I heard that the gas bottle had exploded. ¡Madre mía! I just wish we had been able to arrest him or shoot him in the first place then this would not have happened. When I heard that he had crashed into you, I couldn't believe it! What are the chances that the suspect from my operation, which you had instigated by your chance meeting with Knox, would months later end up crashing into your car by complete accident. That bastard Mason! Charlotte told me you were just taking new gas bottles to your houseboat. It is unbelievable! Unbelievably unlucky. I didn't really believe in God or fate or anything like that before but now, I think I might," said Ramon, becoming quite animated.

"I know. I'm struggling with it myself. I don't know if Charlotte has told you but until earlier I wasn't able to remember much of anything but just today...sorry Ramon, did you say Mason? You said Mason crashed into my car."

"Sorry, I forgot your memory has not been great. That's right Mason, Tony Mason crashed into your car, which was being chased by police. He was the kingpin of the drug operation, the one who sent Jimmy Knox over here."

"I still can't remember the crash itself and Charlotte and the doctor told me the circumstances yesterday but neither mentioned the name of the driver and you have never told me the name of the guy behind all this."

"You know, I think you are right, because as much as I trust and respect you, I didn't tell anyone other than my own team and the tactical support teams until the day of the operation. Obviously Interpol and the NCA were the ones who told me about him. He was named and his photograph was shown on local television that day but I remember your phone call just before the crash. I was going to text you his details and send you his photograph but I never did because the call came through that he had hijacked the car. Wait a minute, Jimmy Knox must have told you his name or you have just forgotten where you heard it."

"I am sure he didn't. You see, the thing is, I had this very realistic dream when I was in a coma. I was in Sunderland, on the Pennywell Estate I think it was. I went to a house and there was a party going on. Things happened at the party and there was a drugs raid. I hid in a garden and had wraps of cocaine and was arrested. Look, I know this sounds as if I am out of my mind and perhaps I am but until you arrived I had convinced myself that my dream was explainable and I had put it to bed, but now I'm not so sure," said James.

"What is that?" asked Ramon, leaning forward to look at James' sketch, which he picked up. "This is a good likeness of him. You have made him look a little younger maybe but I could identify Mason from this. So you must have heard his name and seen his photograph. Maybe he was with Knox when you went to Sunderland and to that pub?" asked Ramon.

James stared at Ramon with incredulity.

"Are you telling me that I have just drawn the face of the real Tony Mason; the guy who crashed into me and who is now dead? The guy who was behind this whole drug operation and who was from Sunderland?"

"Yes, I think so," said Ramon, looking at the drawing from different distances. "Yes, it is him. You have a talent for this by the way," he continued.

"My head is spinning. I can't take this in. Let me think for a minute. There has to be a rational explanation for this but one thing I know is you did NOT tell me his name. I thought you wanted to keep that information confidential and I understood, so I didn't press you for it. Knox did not mention his name. No, I have no idea but look at the page behind the sketch," said James, forcefully.

Ramon turned the page and read down the list of words and phrases and looked up at James and shrugged his shoulders.

"I cannot help you amigo. We will find out soon, I'm sure of it. In the meantime, I think I should go. You need to be relaxing if you are going to get better," said Ramon, standing up to leave, as he could see the revelation was making James agitated.

"Wait, Ramon, please. I will be thinking about this all day unless I can work this out. I did not see any television report on Mason. Did it show his photo?" asked James.

"Yes, it did. Wait a minute," said Ramon, bringing out his mobile phone. James watched him scrolling through screens on his phone and he then held up James' drawing. "Yes, there is definitely a strong resemblance. Here, look for yourself," he said, passing the phone and the sketch to James.

He looked at the photo on Ramon's mobile phone. It was a police mugshot of Tony Mason. Then James looked at his detailed sketch of the face. It was the same man, albeit in his eyes, although Mason was perhaps ten years younger in the dream.

"How old was Mason?" he asked.

"He was thirty-five, I think, yes thirty-five," replied Ramon.

"When was this photo taken?"

"It is recent. Maybe six months ago, when he got out of prison."

"In my dream, Ramon, he was younger and that is why I have drawn him like that. This makes it even weirder. You were able to tell it was him from my drawing. Unbelievable! What actually happened during the Op?" asked James.

"Okay. Okay. Everything was going well. They had brought two out of the three containers back to their warehouse at the far end of the docks. We had snipers and several tactical support teams who are well-trained, like your SAS, and the lorry was going back for the last one. I thought Mason and all the others were in the warehouse. I gave the order to go and there was shooting in the warehouse. That is where Knox, who was an NCA informant by the way, was shot. We realised that Mason was still in the cab of the lorry, which had just left the warehouse. Police approached it and he just emptied two clips from a sub-machine gun into two police cars, killing a young officer and hitting two more. It was a black day for me. I have never lost a man in the course of an operation and I hope I never will again. The drugs seizure, no matter how big it was, was not worth a life. The olivar in Biniaraix was stormed at the same time, so we now have three men on remand due to go to court soon. They are pleading guilty and will get long prison sentences, especially because firearms were used and my officer died, even though it was this guy here who killed him," said Ramon, nodding towards the sketch.

Once you are back on your feet, you need to give me a statement about what you remember and we will need to sort out a criminal injury claim. You need to get a new car and something for all the pain you have gone through."

"All in good time," said James, handing Ramon back his mobile phone.

"Now it really is time for me to go. Don't get up," said Ramon smiling, as he stood up. "¡Hasta luego amigo! ¡Mejórate pronto! Adiós."

"Adiós Ramon y gracias," said James, waving to Ramon as he left his room.

James was once again alone with his thoughts. He turned to the page with his words and looked at them. He then lifted his android mobile phone and went onto Google Maps on the internet and searched 'Pennywell Estate' and 'Hillingdon Street'. Hillingdon Street in Sunderland was a real street and was indeed located on the Pennywell Estate. He checked the likely route that the taxi would have taken when driving him to the pub near the Stadium of Light football ground, coming from Newcastle Airport. It was nowhere near there. He thought it unlikely that he would have seen signs for either the estate or the street.

James decided not to mention this to Charlotte. He didn't want it to ruin the visit. Anyway, it was possible that his judgement was being distorted by the fact that he was on pain relief medication and he had received a severe trauma to his head. He thought it would be wise to take it all with a pinch of salt until he felt much better.

Charlotte and his sons arrived an hour later and all three were in a cheery mood, which made James forget about his dream.

"Your hair looks nice. Did you have it done this morning?" asked James of Charlotte.

"Yes I did. Thank you for noticing. I went in to see Scottish Johnny at Viktoria earlier. It's really lovely there now. You know there's a café and they sell some really tasteful homeware. I was telling him the good news and he said, 'Tell James from me I'm so happy to hear the news and I'll catch up for a drink with him in Bar Blue when he's better'. He has also very kindly sent you this. It's their delicious tarta de almendras," said Charlotte, producing a cake from her wicker shopping bag.

"That was nice of him. He's a nice guy, Johnny," said James. "I'm looking forward to getting back on my feet. One thing I am going to do for us when I get better is book us a week on *Soul*. We are going to have a week off from the hotel. We can do it over Christmas. The wood-burning stove will keep us warm. We can eat nice food, drink good wine, play games and go for bracing walks!" said James with vigour.

"Can I drink wine too, Daddy?" asked Rueben.

"Why not?" said James, nodding.

He looked at his family and was thankful for them and vowed to try and relax and enjoy them more than ever.

Chapter 15

The Big Question

It was now several weeks since James had been discharged from hospital. He had ended up staying almost two weeks after waking from his coma as Jésus, his doctor, had wanted to monitor him. He was worried about the swelling to James' brain but it finally reduced enough for him to be satisfied. James had been going back for weekly check-ups since leaving hospital and Jésus was now happy that there didn't appear to be any significant lasting damage to his brain or motor functions. James had returned to work at the hotel but was easing himself back in and was now up to a four-day week instead of his usual five.

Today was Friday and James had the day off, so he collected Reuben from school in Sóller and they walked back to the plaça. Some of Reuben's school friends and other friends from the village were playing, so James returned home with his Reuben's schoolbag, leaving his son to play. Reuben and several of his friends were playing hide and seek. He was trying to hide behind a large tree in the middle of the plaça. His friend Ole, who was the seeker was getting very close to finding him, when all of a sudden, a little boy who Reuben had never seen before, stood in front of him in his crouching position, allowing him to remain uncompromised and Ole ran off to look elsewhere.

Reuben turned to the little boy, who appeared to be about his age and said, "Gracias."

The boy just nodded and smiled. Reuben smiled back at the boy, who he thought looked a little sad and dirty. His clothes and appearance were somewhat dishevelled. Before Reuben had a chance to ask the boy if he wanted to join them in the game, he walked off.

Later, after his lunch, Reuben returned to the plaça and was sitting by the water fountain, waiting for his friends to return. He looked down the street and saw the same boy from earlier. He watched as the boy seemed very interested in an open window of a house that was accessible from the footpath.

What's he doing? That's Molly's house, he thought to himself.

He then saw the boy lean in and then stand up, putting several dark, round items, which looked a bit like apples to Reuben, inside his jumper. He saw him lean in for a second time and bring out another one, which he then saw the boy take a bite of, whilst looking all around. He didn't appear to have seen Reuben and he then walked back down the street in the direction of Sóller.

Reuben felt sorry for the boy. He realised that the boy had just stolen some of Molly's renowned scotch eggs from her window sill.

He must have been really hungry, thought Reuben, *judging by the speed at which he ate the first one.*

Reuben had a dilemma. He knew he should go and tell Molly that the boy had just stolen her scotch eggs, or at least go and tell his dad, but he couldn't bring himself to do it. Five minutes had passed and none of his friends had reappeared, so, just as he was going to call on one or two, as he got up he noticed the boy was hiding in a little alleyway further down the street. He decided to go and investigate and wandered down the street until he came close to the boy, who on seeing Reuben jumped to his feet and started to run away.

Reuben called after him, "Wait! Wait! I just want to see if you are okay."

The boy looked around as he ran and then stopped. He looked back at Reuben, who was now walking towards him. The boy looked nervous. He was still holding a half-eaten scotch egg.

Reuben said, "My name is Reuben. Do you speak English? ¿O hablas Español?"

The boy just looked at him for a few seconds and then said quietly,

"I name Adnan. English, a little speak."

"Where are you from?" asked Reuben.

"I from Aleppo, Syria," said Adnan.

Reuben realised that Adnan must be from one of several refugee families that had just arrived in the Sóller Valley. He had been learning about the fighting in Syria in school, because his teacher had told his class that they were getting a new classmate the following week from Syria.

"Are you going to school here soon?" asked Reuben slowly and deliberately.

Adnan shrugged his shoulders and looked at the ground.

"I do not say. I am here in Sóller with mother and sister but Adnan run away because Adnan sad. Adnan not see father in one year."

Reuben put his hand on his shoulder but recoiled a little from the smell as he got closer. Adnan saw the expression on Reuben's face and said,

"Adnan run and fall in shit of dog. Sorry for smell."

Reuben laughed at his turn of phrase and said,

"You can be my friend. You know 'friend'?"

Adnan nodded and then finished the remainder of his last scotch egg.

"I saw you take those. You must have been very hungry," said Reuben.

"Adnan very hungry and saw big falafels near window. You friend?"

"Adnan, I won't tell but you must go home to your mother. She will be worried, you know 'sad'," said Reuben.

"Okay. Okay. Adnan go home to mother. See you Dell Boy," he said, calling back to Reuben.

Just then Reuben turned to see his father approaching.

"There you are. Haven't you got some homework to do before tea?" asked James.

"Yes. Alright, I'll do it now," he sighed.

Both started walking back home.

"Who was that wee chap? I haven't seen him before," asked James.

"His name is Adnan. He is from one of the Syrian refugee families who have moved into Sóller. I was telling you before that we are getting some new kids at our school but I just met him today for the first time. Dad, can I ask you something and you won't be cross?" asked Reuben tentatively.

"I'll do my best. Go ahead."

"If you saw someone do something and you knew it was wrong, would you always need to tell a grown up?"

"Well, it depends what it is. I would normally say yes but sometimes there are exceptions to the rule. If you have seen something, you can tell me. I promise not to get cross," said James softly.

"Okay. Well I saw Adnan take some scotch eggs from Molly's house. He reached in and grabbed them and ate them really fast. He was really hungry. You see, he told me he had run away from home because he was very sad because he hadn't seen his dad for a year. I told him that he must go back to his mum in Sóller and he said he would. You are not mad at him are you?"

"No. I'm not mad at him, Reuben. At the same time if he has really run away from home we need to let the police know where you saw him so they can make sure he's safe, and I will have a quiet word with Molly. Don't worry I will not get him into trouble. Okay?"

"Okay. Thanks, Dad."

They returned home and James contacted the Policía Local in Sóller to inform them that he had seen a potential missing boy and he was happy to hear that he had been reported missing but had returned home of his own volition and had been reunited with his mother.

The following morning, James got up after having had very little sleep. He had been thinking about his dream and the car crash. He had remembered the events leading up to it. He had tried for weeks to put the whole episode behind him but he didn't have closure. The previous night it had resurfaced again while he was trying to sleep. He remembered driving to Palma and making a call to Ramon. He recalled the call being cut short and noticing lots of police at most road junctions in the area. He relived in his head seeing a dark-coloured car heading towards him at speed and the blinding lights shining in his eyes and that was it. The next thing he woke up in hospital. It was the vivid dream and the 'coincidences', as he was now calling them to himself, that kept him awake the previous night.

After a late breakfast, he decided to take the bull by the horns once and for all, for his own sanity, if nothing else. He went to his study and got onto his computer and typed in, 'Police stations near Pennywell Estate, Sunderland.' The result came up and he decided to ring Sunderland West Police Station and speak to someone, anyone who might be able to put his mind to rest. Initially he thought it might be more appropriate to e-mail with a full explanation but wondered how he would word such a thing. He decided to ring.

After being taken through numerous options, the phone was answered by a female.

"Sunderland West Police Station. What's the nature of your call?"

"I'd like to speak to someone in CID or the drug squad, please."

"Is it to report a crime?"

"I am a former police officer and I live overseas now. I just need to speak to anyone who is familiar with the Pennywell Estate and Tony Mason," said James.

"I hear that bugger got killed in Majorca a few weeks ago, pet. Look, I tell you what, so this isn't official police business?" asked the switchboard operator.

"No. I was an ex-detective in the Met and the RUC and I know I shouldn't be given information over the phone but if I could just ask someone in the drug squad a couple of non-sensitive questions, it would really help me. Tony Mason crashed into my car in Mallorca; that's how he died."

"Alright pet, what's your name?" asked the operator.

"James. James Gordon."

"This is what I am going to do for you. All the detectives are at a big scene at the moment. I was in the drug squad here for the last five years of my service and I retired last year and came back to do the phones. I am on my break in about ten minutes. I will ring you back on your number there and you can ask me and I'll tell you what I know. Alright pet?"

"That's very kind of you. I appreciate that. What's your name?"

"I'm Barbara, James. I'll talk shortly. Bye."

James waited by the phone with a list of questions. The phone rang a short time later.

"Hello, James Gordon speaking."

"Hello James, it's Barbara here. What is it you want to know?" she asked.

"Thanks for getting back to me Barbara. Right, first of all, do you have a Detective Sergeant Billy McWhirter at your station or neighbouring stations? He would be in his fifties, short grey hair, slim build and about five feet ten."

"No. That name doesn't ring a bell, pet. Wait a minute. Does he have a big grey moustache?" she asked hopefully.

"No, not when I saw him."

"The thing is, I think there was a DS McWhirter in drug squad before my time but I think he retired about eight or nine years ago. I don't know his first name. I have heard people talk about him but only by his nickname, which was Tash. When did you meet him?"

"That's the thing. I'm not sure when it was. Let's say it could have been ten years ago," said James, not wanting to tell her the truth, as he knew it would sound ridiculous.

"I never met him James but I know there is a photo of him in the station on the wall, when he played cricket for Northumbria Police. I can scan it and e-mail it to you if you like, pet."

"That would be great Barbara. Now, I've got some more questions for you before you do that. Would you be able to find out if DS McWhirter ever arrested and charged Tony Mason for possession of cocaine? Next, did Mason hang out in any houses in Hillingdon Street? Now this could have been ten years ago. Did Mason have a girlfriend around that time? She would have been mid-twenties, long blonde hair and a pretty girl. That's the last question," said James.

"Can I ask you why you want to know this James? I understood what you said earlier, that Mason crashed into you in Majorca, isn't that right?" she asked.

"That part I can confirm. Barbara, I was in a coma for two and a half weeks and during that time I had a very vivid dream. This is just helping me get closure with some things. That's as much as I can say."

"Alright, pet. I understand. Okay, what's your e-mail address?"

"It's jgordon67@gmail.com," he answered.

"You can buy me a large drink for this pet, if you're ever over in the north- east. It might take me a day or two because I will have to check old custody records. No wait, my mate Dave is on duty tonight and he's a whiz with computers. All the records have been computerised. Leave it with me pet. Take care, bye."

James came off the phone feeling glad he had made the call and lucky to have found someone as helpful and obliging as Barbara. He left his study and started to prepare the evening meal. He hoped Barbara might send him some answers in a couple of days. After dinner, he sat down with a glass of wine and was half way through an episode of a Danish crime series called *The Killing*, when the phone rang. He could hear Charlotte answer the phone and then she walked in to the living room and handed the phone to him saying,

"It's someone called Barbara with a strong Geordie accent."

James was surprised and set his glass of wine down and pressed the pause button on his remote.

"Hi Barbara. I wasn't expecting to hear from you so soon."

"I hope I'm not disturbing you. I only remembered you are an hour ahead of us here after I spoke to that lady, who I'm presuming is your wife," she started.

"It's fine Barbara. Go ahead."

"I'm just letting you know I have sent you an e-mail with a couple of photos attached. The first is a blown-up copy of DS McWhirter from about fifteen years ago. The second photo is of a girl who used to run about with Mason for a few years on and off up until about five years ago. Her name was Chrissy Mitchell. It might be her that you described. She's dead now. She died a few years ago from a heroin overdose, I gather. In relation to Mason's arrests, my mate Dave very kindly checked his arrests on computer. There are several occasions when McWhirter arrested Mason but you mentioned Hillingdon Street. There is a custody record from November, 2007, a few years before Mason did five years for drug importation and he was arrested in a garden in Hillingdon Street, Sunderland with a quantity of cocaine in his possession. The arresting officer was a Police Constable Murphy, who I knew. He's off the job now but everyone called him Smurf. It did say that DS McWhirter was the officer in charge of the case and he charged him. That's everything."

"Barbara, you are an absolute star. I really appreciate the work you put in for me. I'm going to go and look at the e-mail and the photos. Listen, I run a small hotel in Mallorca, in a lovely village called Fornalutx and if you ever want a few days in Mallorca you can stay in my hotel with fifty per cent discount. I will send you our website address and you can see how lovely the area is, but in the meantime, thank you very much indeed for this. I really appreciate it," said James.

"Oh don't mention it, pet. When you are in our job it is nice to help other 'ex-job' members, especially given the fact that Tony Mason put you in a coma. I had dealings with him myself James and we had a party here when we heard about his death. He was a nasty bastard who brought nothing but evil and despair everywhere he went. The sad thing is, as I'm sure you know, some other bastard will already have taken his place, excuse my French. Anyway pet, I hope you find what you are looking for and tell your wife I'm sorry for ringing so late. Bye pet, bye."

James quickly walked down to his study and switched on the computer and opened up his e-mail. He looked at the first photo, which was of DS McWhirter, and even though it was of a man sitting in a team photograph wearing cricket whites and sporting a grey moustache, he recognised him as being the detective from his dream. He was frightened but also curious to open the second attachment. He opened it and there was a police photograph taken after the charge of Chrissy Mitchell. It was a mugshot-type photo of her face from 2007 but James froze, as he instantaneously recognised this girl as the girl at the party in his dream. His heart was pounding. He had no rational explanation for what had happened to him.

Just then, Charlotte walked into the study.

"I'm off to bed. Are you coming up?" she asked.

"Yeah. I'll be up in a minute," he said, looking towards her.

"Who was that on the phone?" she asked.

"No-one really. It's too late to start talking about it now," said James sighing.

"Is everything alright? James tell me. I have a right to know. What's wrong?" she asked, sitting beside him.

"I don't know how to explain it because I don't understand it myself. Okay, I'll try. When I was in a coma, I had a very vivid dream. I could describe the house I went to, the wallpaper, the carpet, the people's faces, everything. I believe it was in an estate in Sunderland. I was doing things that would be out of character for me. Then, there was a police raid; a drugs raid. I was arrested and taken to a police station. I was interviewed and charged. They kept calling me by a different name: Tony Mason. I asked for a mirror because I said I am James Gordon. I looked in the mirror and I saw the face of a younger man, not me. I have that face embedded in my brain. Tony Mason is the name of the guy who crashed into me, the guy who died at the scene. I was never told his name until Ramon came to see me the day after I got out of the coma. That morning, I sketched the face I had seen looking back at me in the mirror. Ramon recognised my sketch as a younger Tony Mason. I had never met him or seen a photo of him before. Ramon showed me his photograph and it was the man I saw in the mirror; the man's face that I drew. I remembered names of police officers. I could visualise the face of a girl at the party. I remembered place names all from places I had never heard of or been to. I haven't been sleeping very well the last couple of nights, so I decided to contact the police station in Sunderland where I believe I was taken to in my dream. Barbara, who rang, was a very nice lady who did some research for me.

"To cut a long story short, she sent me photos of a police detective, whose face I remember like it was yesterday, and that of a girl. I have just downloaded them and in my head I recognise these people from my dream. I even wrote the name of this detective sergeant down on my notepad in hospital. He retired about nine years ago but he charged Mason with possession of drugs exactly like in my dream. The girl in my dream looked exactly like the girl in the photo Barbara sent me, who was Mason's one-time girlfriend. She died about five years ago. I waited until I was off the medication before I pursued this further and if I am honest, I was a little worried to look into it, because I thought the accident may have caused me serious memory issues or worse, that I was developing mental illness. I'm not saying that I think I was really there in person but somehow I have mentally gained a first-hand insight into an evening that Mason had about ten years ago," said James sighing.

"Why didn't you tell me all this earlier?" said Charlotte, putting her hand on his shoulder to comfort him. "Look, I don't have an explanation for this any more than you have. Sometimes the mind can play tricks on you or perhaps when you were technically dead for that minute, something happened at the same time he died. He was only a couple of feet from you after all. All I know is you, or I, or anyone else will not be able to give you a rational explanation that you will be happy to accept. I know you. You have often told me, 'I work on evidence. Show me the evidence.' Well I'm afraid you may have found the evidence but the evidence to what? That is the problem. I thought you were gone. Your sons, I fear, thought you were gone, even though I was trying to be as positive as I could be. You have been given a second chance, so please wake up to that fact and put everything else behind you."

James sat for a moment, thinking about what he had just heard.

"You know me too well. You are right. It doesn't matter if this was God or a higher being, or just something in the deepest recesses of my brain getting tangled up with Mason's brain. As you say, we will never know. You are right that I like to see evidence but my gut instinct has served me well over the years and my gut instinct tells me everything happens for a reason. What that reason is, I don't know for sure but I am going with my gut on this one. It is telling me that I have been spared. It wasn't my time to go and yes, that is a leap of faith. Maybe I was getting a privileged look at what my life could have been like if I had lived it differently. All I know is, I am extremely fortunate to be here at all. We are privileged to live in such a beautiful part of the world and we have our boys and each other. This has certainly been a wake-up call for me: not to take things for granted or to be complacent. Thanks for listening. Now let's go to bed," said James, feeling a burden had been lifted from his shoulders.

He went to bed feeling content and newly invigorated with life. He felt he now had closure on trying to understand what had happened to him. He wasn't quite ready for paradise just yet. He still had a lot of living to do in his paradise on earth that was for him Fornalutx and the Sóller Valley.